DOCTOR WHO
PARADISE TOWERS

Based on the BBC television series by Stephen Wyatt by
arrangement with BBC Books, a division of BBC Enterprises Ltd

STEPHEN WYATT

Number 134 in the
The Doctor Who Library

A TARGET BOOK
published by
the Paperback Division of
W.H. Allen & Co. Plc

A Target Book
Published in 1988
By the Paperback Division of
W.H. Allen & Co. Plc
44 Hill Street, London W1X 8LB

Novelisation copyright © Stephen Wyatt, 1989
Original script copyright © Stephen Wyatt, 1987
'Doctor Who' series copyright © British Broadcasting
Corporation, 1987, 1989

The BBC producer of *Paradise Towers* was John Nathan-Turner
The director was Nick Mallett
The role of the Doctor was played by Sylvester McCoy

Printed and bound in Great Britain by
Cox & Wyman Ltd, Reading

ISBN 0 426 20330 5

CONTENTS

1	The Last of the Yellow Kangs	7
2	No Visitors	19
3	Tea and Cakes	29
4	The Chief	41
5	This Way and That	55
6	Brainquarters	68
7	Come into My Parlour	77
8	The Illustrated Prospectus	89
9	The Basement	105
10	The Pool in the Sky	113
11	Kroagnon	127
12	Farewells	142

1

The Last of the Yellow Kangs

It was Mel who first of all wanted to visit Paradise Towers. She felt after some very arduous adventures recently she was entitled to relax by a swimming pool – a beautiful indoor pool with heated water and marble floors and luxurious chairs by its side. She talked so longingly about it that the Doctor deeply regretted having had to jettison the pool from the TARDIS because it had started to leak. And, one day, flicking through the images in an old travel video-brochure she found lying around the TARDIS, she came across pictures of Paradise Towers.

The building itself was impressive enough. A huge tower block forming a separate man-made planet with soaring white towers that gleamed in the sun and brightly coloured streets and squares, where fountains played and exotic flowers bloomed. Apartments to live in which were spacious and spotless, stuffed full of remarkable devices to make the business of daily life easier. Well-planned offices from which those in charge of this artificially created paradise could ensure its smooth running. Mel thought that living there must be like being perpetually on holiday. And that was before she had even seen the pool. When she finally saw its shimmering blue water and the lovely rich tones of its surroundings, it quite took her breath away.

'Look, Doctor, look,' she exclaimed excitedly. 'There it is, right at the very top of that wonderful tall building. I can't wait to have a dip in that.'

The Doctor had had other plans but he realised that it would be useless to argue, not to mention rather selfish. And so the

TARDIS was soon hurtling through time and space towards Paradise Towers.

Mel could hardly take her eyes off the pictures of the pool nonetheless. It seemed so long since she'd been able to relax in warm, soothing water. The Doctor, to be honest, became a little irritated with her enthusiasm.

'I think that's enough of that, Mel,' he announced.

'Why?' Mel enquired. 'It looks great.'

The Doctor pursed his lips. 'Well, if you want to stay here watching a guide book when you could actually be enjoying the real thing, that's up to you.'

Mel turned to him excitedly. 'You mean we're nearly there?'

The Doctor nodded. 'You may want to lie by the pool and do nothing all day. I intend to explore. Paradise Towers is supposed to be a remarkable architectural achievement, I believe. It won all sorts of awards back in the twenty-first century.' He moved towards the TARDIS's control panel. 'Well, are you ready?'

'Ready?' Mel replied, eyes shining. 'I can't wait.'

As he prepared for landing, the Doctor gave an inward sigh. When he thought of all the really exciting planets they could be visiting, he did feel a little cheated that they had to go somewhere as bland and perfect as Paradise Towers. That was the trouble with the young, he mused, they had no real spirit of adventure. So he imagined a peaceful, uneventful few days stretching ahead of the two of them. He could not, of course, have been more wrong.

The last of the Yellow Kangs ran down Potassium Street as fast as her feet could carry her. She knew the street well with its distinctive blue walls, grimy and covered in Kang wallscrawl, its ornate blue street lamps all damaged or smashed completely, the ones remaining flickering eerily, its pavements covered in all manner of refuse: animal, vegetable and mineral. She had been down the street many times in happier days when the other Yellow Kangs had not yet been made unalive and they had beaten the Blue Kangs and the Red Kangs again and again in the never-ending game. Now she was alone. One by one the other Yellow Kangs had gone from her, often without warning, always without explanation. Perhaps it was the fault of the Red Kangs. Or the Blue Kangs. She wasn't sure but somehow she doubted it. There was something else far worse than other Kangs, she suspected, and often at night, when she slept alone in the ominously empty Yellow Kang Brainquarters, she would wake up, sweating and terrified, believing it would come for her too.

On and on she ran. In the distance she could hear a familiar chant, echoing down the deserted street. 'Yellow Kangs are cowardly cutlets,' it went. 'Yellow Kangs are cowardly cutlets . . .' Over and over again. Maybe the Red Kangs had lost track of her. She hoped so. It would be useless to try and explain to any of them what had happened to the other Yellow Kangs or to beg for an end to the game for a while. They would go on playing it to the end of time. The Blue Kangs too. And she would have to keep on trying to escape from them, whatever else frightened or puzzled her. Not that there was time for thought now. She must keep on running down Potassium Street until she had lost her pursuers and could creep into Yellow Kang Brainquarters without detection.

'Yellow Kangs are cowardly cutlets . . . Yellow Kangs are cowardly cutlets . . .' Was it her imagination or were the Red Kangs catching up with her? She thought she had double-backed successfully leaving them futilely running down Nitrate Street in the wrong direction. But their voices certainly sounded nearer. She must hurry.

And then suddenly she stumbled over something and fell. For a moment she was too startled to move and then, when she tried to get up, she realised that the lonely anxieties of the last few weeks, the sleepless nights and the unfinished meals had taken their toll. She could not go on even if she wanted to. She must stay and let the Red Kangs come if they must. Let them win the game if they wanted. It didn't seem to matter any more. She no longer had the energy to play. All she could do was crawl wearily towards the nearest doorway and take refuge within it, drawing breath exhaustedly.

She listened carefully. A Kang needed acute hearing to cope with life in the Towers and she owed her survival in part to that. Red Kang voices came from a nearby crossroads. They were close but not as close as she had feared.

'Yellow Kangs are cowardly cutlets . . .'

The voices were still mocking and defiant but she sensed that the Red Kangs were losing hope of finding her this time. They had followed her trail so far but no longer knew which way to go. To her relief, the chanting became more ragged and then died away completely. She strained to hear what they would say next.

'Leave her for another day. Cowardly cutlet!' came one voice.

'Leave her for the Cleaners,' came another and the comment was followed by raucous laughter. It was a saying all the Kangs used, a threat, but not a serious one, to scare the more timid and childish girls. It meant nothing, the Yellow Kang thought. Except that the Red Kangs were abandoning the game and returning to their Brainquarters. She was safe for another day.

She listened eagerly as their voices and footsteps receded away into the distance down Sodium Street towards Sunrise Square. Perhaps she was listening too eagerly. Otherwise she might have been alerted sooner to another sound, low at first, growing in volume as it came nearer. A soft mechanical whirring, regular but somehow menacing.

By the time she had heard the sound it was too late. She could only look up at the approaching shape first in disbelief then in horror as it came closer and closer. Even if she could have found a last ounce of energy to run it would have been useless. She could only watch, mesmerised. The noise, barely detectable at first, now deafened her. She knew there was no hope. And yet she started to scream. And scream. Until the screaming was cut short and the last of the Yellow Kangs was unalive.

A crude scrawl had been drawn by another Kang on the wall

10

just near where she fell. A scrawl which might have given her warning of what was to happen to her. It showed a girl dressed in yellow threatened by two large, white mechanical claws.

'Well, here we are,' the Doctor announced. Mel waited expectantly as the door of the TARDIS opened. The TARDIS will have materialised in one of those sumptuous looking squares, she thought. Fountain of Happiness perhaps or the Grotto of Delight. Then it would be up to the top floor for a dip in the pool. The TARDIS door opened noisily. That was the first indication something was wrong. But there was worse to come.

Mel stared out of the open door in horror. She could not really believe her eyes. The TARDIS had materialised amid a heap of junk. The noise was its door scraping along a mass of cans and discarded scrap metal. That was that explained. But was what she was looking at really part of Paradise Towers? Perhaps they'd come to the wrong place. The Doctor had been known to make mistakes in the past.

The Doctor, however, was already through the door and Mel hurried to follow him. As they advanced out of the TARDIS, their feet were scrunching on all manner of rubbish lying on the outside floor. The Doctor was immediately all curiosity. He upended a battered cardboard box and a couple of large rats scuttered away. 'Intelligent little creatures,' he murmured appreciatively.

Mel, however, was too busy taking in the awfulness of their surroundings. And though she would have liked there to have been a mistake, she knew there hadn't been one. Because she could just about recognise this was one of the squares in Paradise Towers so lovingly described in the video-brochure. Fountain of Happiness Square, she suspected. But changed immeasurably for the worst. The floor was covered in rubbish. The walls looked as if they had not been cleaned for decades. And indeed the only splash of brightness in the whole drab, dirty square was the highly coloured graffiti that had been daubed over them by some childish hand. The large glass windows that let daylight in were smashed in numerous places and the splinters of glass had joined the rest of the debris on the ground. Saddest of all, perhaps, was the Fountain of Happiness itself. The water had clearly dried up ages ago and the beautiful bowl into which the water used to pour was now rust-stained, cracked and filled with litter. It was difficult to imagine a more desolate and depressing environment and Mel's immediate reaction was to get straight back into the TARDIS.

'You don't happen to know another planet with a swimming pool, do you?' she asked the Doctor. But something about the way he was poking excitedly with his umbrella among the junk told her he was not going to be that helpful.

'There is a rather spectacular swimming pool on the planet Griophos, I understand,' he replied airily, examining the yellowing paper collecting in the fountain.

'We could try there then,' said Mel eagerly. The Doctor looked dubious.

'There's just one snag, Mel. It's for the exclusive use of the Gulmeres.'

'Who are they?'

'A rather nasty breed of flesh-eating octupi.' He returned to his exploration. 'Personally, I'd rather stay here and explore. I wonder what's happened.'

Mel looked round dispiritedly. 'It's got awful, that's what happened.' She sighed and decided to get the better of her disappointment. 'Still, now we're here, I suppose I might as well see what the pool's like,' she conceded.

'That's the spirit, Mel,' the Doctor returned approvingly. 'This could be fascinating.' He started off across Fountain of Happiness Square towards one of the dingy, ill-lit streets that led off it, pausing only to turn back briefly towards Mel. 'Are you coming?'

'All right,' Mel agreed, now secretly determined not to miss out on any of the adventure. 'But one thing, Doctor. If anything goes wrong and we get separated, we'll meet at the pool all right?' She knew the Doctor and she knew the situations they could get themselves in. The Doctor was a masterly improviser, of course, as well as an intrepid explorer, but during her time with him, it had sometimes occured to Mel that a little more forward planning might have helped. Here was a chance.

'Oh, very well,' the Doctor sighed, his mind already racing on to investigating all the ins and outs of the Towers. 'But we've only just arrived. There's no need to start worrying yet.'

An experienced Time Traveller should have known better. No sooner were the confident words out of his mouth than a strange metal arrow whizzed through the air from a place of concealment in the Square. And, before the Doctor could say another word, the arrow had pinned him neatly by his coat to the adjacent wall. Just a split second later, another arrow whizzed across the Square and pinned Mel there too. Other arrows aimed with equal accuracy followed. They were pinned still more tightly to the wall. Both of them tried to struggle free but it was hopeless. They were as incapable of moving as flies trapped in a spider's web. Mel just hoped that the comparison wasn't too accurate. She had no desire to be anybody's dinner. She peered anxiously about her as they waited for their assailants to emerge from the shadows and show their faces.

Caretaker number 345 stroke 12 subsection 3 was not a happy man. In fact, he was a rather frightened man. He was one of the younger, more able-bodied Caretakers so he was always being given the job of patrolling the more dangerous and distant streets of Paradise Towers. Every time he had applied to be put on to an easier, less alarming job, the Chief had been less than sympathetic, fluently quoting whole sections of the rule book at him to prove he had to what he was told. And in the end, it was impossible to argue with the Chief. He knew the rule book backwards and had an answer for every complaint or problem a Caretaker could bring to him. So here he was again on the Potassium Street beat.

There were nasty rumours about what had been happening in the Potassium Street area. The young Caretaker, if he was honest, had seen nothing in the three weeks he'd had the job – but that didn't alter the fact that the last Caretaker on this particular beat had mysteriously disappeared. At least the young Caretaker had seen nothing of him since taking over. He was never at the Caretakers' Headquarters. The Chief would have none of these worries, of course. 'He's been transferred to other duties,' he announced firmly, holding up the rule book. 'all according to paragraph 12 of Rule 79b.' There was no answer to the rule book. All the Caretakers knew that.

The young Caretaker made his way carefully down Potassium Street looking nervously about him, his Mark 12 LDCE (Long Distance Communication Expediter) in his hand. Half of him expected to be attacked at any moment. And half of him knew that it was silly to doubt the wisdom of the Chief. Or the rule book.

It was time to report to the Chief. The Chief expected regular reports at every inter-section and the young Caretaker knew better than to disappoint him. He raised his Mark 12 LDCE, pressed a button and announced his name and number. There was a slight crackle and then he heard the bright, confident tones of the Chief Caretaker.

'We are receiving you, Caretaker number 345 stroke 12 subsection 3. Make your report.'

The young Caretaker took a deep breath. 'I am proceeding along Potassium Street,' he reported, 'corridor 5673 section 201 opposite door 782 on floor 35 north side.' He looked up at the wall nearest to where he was standing and tutted disparagingly over the brightly coloured scribble that almost covered it. 'Considerable evidence of wallscrawl all along this part of street, Chief. Wallscrawlers obviously active here. Over.'

'Report noted,' the Chief's voice replied. 'Proceed now to report on corridor 5673 section 301.'

'Yes, Chief.' The young Caretaker sighed. Orders were orders but still he wished he could be back in the comfort of Caretaker Headquarters not out tramping the streets of Paradise Towers for another couple of hours. He could be fired at by Wallscrawlers. Or bothered by Rezzies with a list of complaints. Or worse.

His foot struck something. He looked down. Lying on the ground was a strip of yellow material. The sort worn for decoration by Yellow Wallscrawlers. He stooped to pick it up and give a closer examination. He might have thought it had just been dropped there while the Wallscrawlers were larking about. Except that the scarf was torn and bloodstained. As if its owner had been attacked brutally.

His hand went immediately to the Mark 12 LDCE. He started to give his number and position but the words wouldn't come. He could only stutter hopelessly.

'We are receiving you, Caretaker number 345 stroke 12 subsection 3.' The Chief's voice was testy now. 'What's the matter?'

'I'm scared, Chief.' It was a tremendous relief to let the words out. The wallscrawls were disturbing enough. Claws attacking Wallscrawlers, Red, Yellow and Blue. But to actually find evidence of the attacks was worse still. His nerve was about to crack and he hoped fervently that the Chief would be sympathetic and let him come back to Headquarters.

'Orders are orders. Number One rule of the Caretakers, Caretaker number 345 stroke 12 subsection 3.' How many times had he heard the Chief say that? More than he could remember. The Chief was not going to listen to his doubts and fears. And could he really blame him? The Chief had far more important things on his mind and the whole smooth running of Paradise Towers to consider. The young Caretaker was a very small cog in the wheel, he knew.

Nevertheless, he made one last try. 'Please, Chief, listen. Something's going wrong. I can feel it's going wrong.' He stared down at the blood-stained yellow scarf he was still holding in his hand. 'Can't I just –?'

'No, Caretaker number 345 stroke 12 subsection 3, you can't.'

There could be no further argument.

Carefully placing the sad remains of the last of the Yellow

Wallscrawlers over his shoulder, the young Caretaker proceeded, as instructed, towards corridor 5673 section 301. It wasn't very far down Potassium Street but in his current tense state it seemed to the young Caretaker miles and miles away.

At first he thought everything was going to be all right after all. The street was quiet and the scrawls on the wall were less scary in what they depicted. To his surprise, he felt himself begin to walk with a more confident stride. All was well until he finally arrived at section 301 and reached for his Mark 12 LDCE to make his report.

The machine started to make a strange bleeping sound he had never heard before. And a lurid flickering light he had never seen before appeared on the dial. A malfunction in the Mark 12 LDCE was very unusual. It was a Caretaker's lifeline and the young Caretaker checked his own regularly. Something had gone very wrong. He pressed the button, desperately trying to make contact with the Chief. 'Chief, are you receiving me?' His voice got ever more desperate. He imagined the Chief's fury at his failure to report in. But all that came from his precious lifeline was still the strange bleep. After a time the sound got through to you.

And then he heard another sound, low at first, growing in volume as it approached. A soft, regular, mechanical whirring. He was not the first to hear it that day but he was not to know that. When it finally registered on his consciousness, he turned his eyes up the Street in the direction of the sound. And froze in horror.

Coming towards him was a large, gleaming white, wheeled robot with headlights and a whole battery of attachments for washing, sweeping, polishing and rubbish collecting. A Robotic Self-Activating Megapodic Mark 7Z Cleaner. The Cleaners, as they were known for short by all the Caretakers except the Chief, who was a stickler for full descriptions and titles at all times, were used for all sorts of menial cleaning tasks around Paradise Towers where a robot was undoubtedly more use than a human being. There had, of course, been rumours that the Cleaners had been getting out of control.

Certain Caretakers had told the young Caretaker in strictest secrecy that they believed the Cleaners had been attacking people. Wallscrawlers mainly but you never knew. After all, the Mark 7Z Cleaners had been fitted with those large mechanical claws . . . Few of the Caretakers believed these stories but this hadn't stopped them being discussed. It helped to pass the time when things were slack.

Looking down at the blood-stained scarf and looking ahead at the Mark 7Z Cleaner, these hushed conversations suddenly took on a new importance for the young Caretaker. The rumours had probably been true all the time. And, far from being cowardly and disloyal, he had actually been right to fear the worst on the Potassium Street beat.

Odd how quickly one can see the truth in a moment of danger. But small consolation to know it with the Cleaner gliding towards him and its menacing white claw shooting out greedily. It was snatching at thin air now but not for long. He had seen the speed the Cleaners could move at and, even if he could have found the energy to run, it would have been useless. His only hope was the Chief. Perhaps the Chief would know how to stop the Cleaner even now. If only he could speak to him.

The LDCE suddenly crackled into life. The Chief's voice was there, asking what he wanted. He explained as best he could with his panic rising and the Cleaner getting nearer by the second. The Chief's voice was calm and reassuring.

'Don't panic, Caretaker number 345 stroke 12 subsection 3 . . .'

'But, Chief . . . it's . . . it's . . .' The enormity of what was happening took away his ability to speak. If the Cleaners were going out of control then who was responsible? The Chief or someone else? And what could anyone hope to gain from killing off Caretakers and Wallscrawlers anyway? The young Caretaker's mind raced through the questions but could find no answers.

And then the white mechanical claw reached out and grabbed him by the throat. He gurgled helplessly and then lapsed into unconsciousness. The last thing he heard was the Chief's voice, still bland and comforting, pouring out words of advice as the Mark 12 LDCE slipped from his fingers. 'Don't worry,' urged the voice. 'Relax and enjoy it.'

A few minutes later the Robotic Self-Activating Megapodic Mark 7Z Cleaner was off once more down Potassium Street heading for a service lift that would take it to the basement of Paradise Towers. The gleaming white Mark 7Z Waste Storage Truck it pulled along behind was clearly very full. Sticking out of it was a foot that had once been part of Caretaker number 345 stroke 12 subsection 3.

2

No Visitors

'Look, what do you want?' The Doctor and Mel were confronting their assailants who now stood confidently in the middle of Fountain of Happiness Square for all to see, staring mockingly at their captives in a none too friendly fashion. It was not very easy to be very authoritative when you were pinned helplessly to a wall like a dead butterfly in a museum display case but the Doctor was doing his best.

They were girls, none of them more than fifteen or sixteen, all dressed in red and carrying strange metallic crossbows, apparently fabricated from the metal debris that littered Paradise Towers. There was, after all, plenty of it to use, Mel thought. The girls all had a wary, proud look. Their long, spiky red hair matched the bright red of their costumes. Tattered and worn though they were, the girls' get-ups reminded Mel of pictures she had seen of Japanese samurai warriors.

'At least tell us who you are,' said the Doctor in growing desperation at the obstinate silence.

'We're the Kangs.' One of the leading girls spoke as if it was the most obvious thing in the galaxy and the captives must be half-witted not to know.

'The Red Kangs,' put in one of her companions proudly. 'Red Kangs are best.' She turned to her companions. 'Who's best?'

'Red Kangs,' they all chorused. 'Red Kangs, Red Kangs are best.'

It was obviously a ritual the Kangs went through. The chanting went on for some time while the Red Kangs pressed in on the Doctor and Mel, crossbows at the ready. By the end a sea of young warlike faces clustered round the Doctor.

19

'So who's best?' demanded the Kang who had lead the chant.

'The Red Kangs, I gather,' returned the Doctor smoothly. 'But there are other coloured Kangs are there?' he added, desperate to change the subject.

'Yeah,' the Kang replied. 'The Blue Kangs. But they're cowardly cutlets.'

'And the Yellow Kangs,' put in another. 'But they're only one now.'

'Why's that?' asked the Doctor.

'Just is.'

'Not got very enquiring minds, have you?' the Doctor remarked sarcastically. He hated it when people failed to show curiosity about what was happening around them. Particularly when, like now, he himself was trying to piece together what was going on.

'Quiet, Doctor.' Mel spoke to try and stop the Doctor's sarcasm annoying the Red Kangs but the actual result was to divert their attention from the Doctor to her.

'You a Kang?' The leading girl eyed her suspiciously.

Mel shook her head. 'No, I'm not a Kang. I'm Mel. And I don't know who the Kangs are.'

'We're Kangs,' the girl returned. 'Red Kangs.'

'Who are, of course, the best,' The Doctor said hastily, in order to prevent another performance of the Red Kang Chant. There was not a male face in sight. A thought occurred to the Doctor. 'Maybe they'll ask you to join up, Mel,' he whispered mischievously.

'I hope not,' Mel replied miserably.

'Bin Liner.' The first Kang who had spoken suddenly cut across their whispers but the words made no immediate sense to either the Doctor or Mel. 'Bin Liner,' she repeated firmly. A response was expected but exactly what response was not clear. Then the penny dropped. She was telling them her name. And after she had done so for the third time, she indicated to the other Red Kangs that they should unpin their two prisoners. Mel hoped this was a good sign not a prelude to something worse.

'Now we're getting somewhere.' The Doctor, freed at last from his undignified pose against the wall, was determined to

20

take the initiative. He raised his hat and putting on one of his most ingratiating smiles, pointed at himself. 'I am the Doctor.'

The other leading Kang stepped forward. 'Fire Escape,' she announced.

'Good names.' This rather banal remark seemed to please the Kangs and the Doctor, growing in confidence, offered his hand to be shaken. But no hand reached out to grasp it. Indeed, the Red Kangs seemed to regard his gesture with great suspicion and even raised their crossbows threateningly again. The Doctor stood there nonplussed.

'I only want to be friendly,' he protested to the still blank faces. 'To say hello,' he added, gesturing frantically to indicate his good intentions.

At some point during the Doctor's performance, to his relief, some of the Kangs obviously realised what he was talking about. 'He wants to how you do,' Fire Escape explained to the slower ones. 'Do we?'

There was a moment's hesitation before the other Kangs gave approval. And then Fire Escape started one of the oddest forms of everyday greeting Mel had ever witnessed. It reminded her of a very slow, rather menacing version of the game of pat-a-cake she used to play at school. She was very thankful that it was the Doctor who would have to respond and not her. Fire Escape was deadly serious during the whole ritual and yet the memory of her childhood games made Mel want to giggle.

The Doctor, however, coped splendidly. He managed to return the greeting exactly, movement for movement, and even added a few flourishes of his own with his hat which seemed to go down rather well with the Kangs. Before very long he had made the full formal acquaintance of not just Bin Liner and Fire Escape but most of the other Kangs as well. Fortunately, it was not necessary, it appeared, to have to go through the whole greeting ceremony with everybody or else the proceedings would have taken a very long time indeed.

'But what about Mel here?' the Doctor enquired when the formalities were over. 'None of the Kangs have said how you do to her.'

21

There was a pause. Fire Escape shook her head. 'You we like, Doctor,' she announced. 'What you wear is high fabshion and icehot for an old one.'

'Thank you very much,' the Doctor replied, not absolutely sure of the exact meaning of these words but getting the general drift. 'But clothes don't maketh the man, you know.'

'No,' agreed Bin Liner. 'But all Kangs have colours. Blue. Yellow. Red. What is Mel's colour?' she turned suspiciously towards Mel, who felt all eyes trained on her now.

'I don't have a colour,' she retorted, stung by the fact that the Kangs had been deliberately ignoring her up till now. 'And I certainly don't want to be a Kang.'

'We don't want you to be a Kang,' Fire Escape snapped back fiercely. 'Not a Red Kang.' It was a cue for the Red Kangs to start their chant again and, much to the Doctor and Mel's dismay, start it they did. The Doctor had to raise his voice to make himself heard over the din. Finally it subsided as quickly as it had begun.

'Look,' the Doctor began when quiet was restored. 'I think now we've been introduced, some explanations are in order. We are visitors to Paradise Towers. Only just arrived. You can't expect Mel to understand what you're talking about.'

'No visitors.' Bin Liner's remark came out so swiftly and so fiercely that the Doctor didn't at first catch its import.

'Pardon?'

'No visitors,' Bin Liner repeated. Again, she seemed to regard the captives as fools for not understanding her. 'No ball games. No flyposts. No visitors.' They were the sort of words Mel was used to seeing on noticeboards back home but Bin Liner was repeating them now with a deadly seriousness.

'You mean visitors aren't allowed?' the Doctor enquired patiently. He hoped that he and Mel were not just about to be punished for infringing some obscure by-law of Paradise Towers.

Bin Liner shook her head. 'No visitors ever.'

'Not since time start,' added Fire Escape.

All was becoming clearer. The Kangs had quite simply never seen any visitors. Mel didn't like to think too closely about what might have happened to any tourists who had been tempted by by seeing the video brochure before her to sample the delights of Paradise Towers. She suspected they had not had the most satisfactory of holidays.

The Doctor meanwhile was thinking more about the present. 'There's always a first time, you know,' he insisted. 'Not everyone you come across is going to be a Kang.'

'No,' Fire Escape agreed. 'There are old ones. And Caretakers. And –'

'Ware tongue!' Bin Liner interrupted fiercely. Fire Escape bit her lip and lapsed into silence.

'And?' The Doctor's eyes were agleam with curiosity. There was nothing more likely to get him interested than discovering something that somebody didn't want him to know. But this time there was no way of finding out what Fire Escape had been about to say. Bin Liner's warning had been enough. The Doctor had to turn his attention to what the Kangs were prepared to tell him. He asked therefore about the Caretakers they had mentioned.

'They wipe away our wallscrawl,' Bin Liner explained. 'Chase us down carrydoors. Catch us if they can.'

'I see,' the Doctor nodded. 'But all the young ones are Kangs?'

'Yes.'

'Young girls I should say, of course,' the Doctor corrected himself. 'There aren't any boys around, are there?'

'Boys?' Fire Escape's face was blank. The other Kangs' faces too. 'What are boys?' Her face wrinkled in puzzlement. The concept was clearly new to her. 'There are old ones, and the Caretakers, and the Kangs and the –' But this time she stopped herself and the Doctor was still none the wiser. He was beginning to suspect there was a strong possibility he would never be. Indeed, he was also beginning to think there was something to be said for Mel's notion of looking for some other planet with a swimming pool. The crossbows were not reassuring. It was time to make an exit. Mel, he noticed, was already trying to edge herself nearer to the TARDIS.

It was worth a try anyway. The Doctor smiled brightly and edged with her. 'Well, I must say, it's been nice meeting you but I think it's time we ought to be on our way. Don't you think so, Mel?'

23

'Yes, Doctor, not a moment to lose,' she agreed heartily. The TARDIS was only some thirty paces away but those thirty paces lay past a whole crowd of Kangs. Mel and the Doctor prepared themselves to run for it. But the Kangs were far too quick. They sensed what their captives were going to do before they even began to do it and blocked their paths. I suppose, the Doctor thought sardonically, when you live in a nightmare like Paradise Towers, you have to learn to act quickly.

'We heard you talk of the pool,' Bin Liner announced, coming right up to the Doctor. Acute hearing too, he noted to himself.

'The great Pool in the Sky.' Fire Escape spoke the words with a great deal of reverence and not a little fear. It was the first indication Mel and the Doctor had that the swimming pool they had so lightly selected might have a much deeper significance for the inhabitants of Paradise Towers. It was useless, however, to try and argue that their overheard conversation had been perfectly harmless. They had said enough to convince the Kangs that they were not to be let go.

'You're coming to our Hide-In.' Bin Liner announced. She gave a gesture of command. Experienced hands grasped them and, before they knew what had happened, the Doctor and Mel had their hands tied neatly and firmly behind their backs. Being bundled up in this way was marginally preferable to being impaled by metal arrows but still didn't make them feel at ease.

'I see the art of knot-tying hasn't died out here anyway,' the Doctor muttered ruefully. 'I wonder if the Blue Kangs behave like this?'

'I thought they liked you,' Mel returned in some puzzlement.

'They liked my clothes,' the Doctor corrected, remembering the Kangs had dubbed them 'high fabshion', whatever that meant. 'It's clearly not enough on its own.'

'Are they tied and true?' Bin Liner had been watching the execution of her orders with an expert eye. The Red Kangs nodded. Fire Escape, meanwhile, was otherwise occupied. The Doctor's ever-inquisitive eye tried to study what she was up to but it wasn't easy with the scrum of Kangs around him. She appeared to be using some sort of telephone. But a phone concealed artfully in a battered old mechanical drinks dispenser. Presumably this was to hide its existence from the Kang's enemies, which appeared to be legion.

Whatever she was hearing on the phone had Fire Escape worried. She summoned Bin Liner over. 'Red Kang Eye-Spy says we can't go through the usual carrydoor. Blue Kangs out and lurking.'

Bin Liner was thoughtful. 'And the Yellows?'

Fire Escape listened again. Her face became grave as she turned to her companion. 'No Yellows. All unalive.'

'All.' Bin Liner echoed her in an awed voice.

'All.' Fire Escape put down the receiver in silence. This was news they had obviously not expected to hear from their lookout and it had taken them by surprise. Suddenly the two girls looked very young and rather frightened.

'Excuse me —' the Doctor called out as politely as he could.

'What?' Fire Escape was again the proud, warlike, ever-vigilant Red Kang, who feared nobody.

'Are you saying a whole tribe of Kangs has been wiped out — er — made unalive — just like that?' The Doctor could not keep the shock out of his voice. Fire Escape nodded her head in agreement. 'But why?' the Doctor pressed. 'You didn't kill them did you?'

The suggestion shocked Fire Escape into speech. 'To make unalive is not part of the Kang game.' She paused and then added with a firmness that was totally convincing. 'No ball games. No flyposts. No wipeouts.'

'Then who does it?' the Doctor urged. 'The Blue Kangs? The Caretakers? Who?'

'It takes place.' Fire Escape would not discuss the subject further. The Doctor sensed much that was unspoken which would only be discussed when he was out of earshot. For the moment, the Red Kang leaders found relief from their worries in frenzied activity. It was time for the band to leave the Square.

'We've been out in the open spaces too long.' Bin Liner was keeping a wary look-out now and the Doctor realised how open to attack they all would be in the Square if any of their foes did

25

appear. The Kangs confused him. They were such an odd mixture of toughness and vulnerability.

'We must go. Ware Blue Kangs.' Fire Escape surveyed the party with its two prisoners, hands well tied, at its centre, all ready now for departure. She raised her hand and made a sign, a sort of blessing or good-luck gesture for the whole group. 'Build High for Happiness.'

'Build High for Happiness.' The other Kangs repeated the gesture and then they were off. Bundled unceremoniously along, up rickety steps and through dingy, ill-smelling corridors, Mel and the Doctor caught only glimpses of what Paradise Towers had become. But it confirmed everything they had feared from that first sight at the door of the TARDIS. The once clean, confidently planned and well-equipped planet was a nightmare of decay and destruction.

'Sorry about the pool, Mel.' They were all crossing a narrow walkway now, high above a litter-strewn square all too like the one they had recently left.

'That's all right, Doctor.' Mel thought it was rather generous of the Doctor to apologise since she was the one who had insisted on coming here in the first place. The leading Kangs were nearly across the walkway now. Ahead was a dark archway. Beyond that it was impossible to see.

'Caretakers! Run!'

Suddenly the whole line of Kangs dissolved and scattered. Just in time those at the front had given the warning. A group of heavily built men in uniforms rushed out of the gloom behind the archway.

'All right, you Wallscrawlers, let's be having you!'

It was lucky for the Kangs that they were young and fit and these men were older and paunchier or they would all have certainly been caught. As it was, the Kangs had to scramble nimbly down stairs or through broken windows to evade them. Mel instinctively followed the other girls. Her tied hands impeded her progress but somehow she found her way back down the stairs and then managed to lose her pursuers in the mass of corridors that led off the square. Kangs were all about her but for

26

the moment none of them had the time or the will to question her or prevent her escape.

She had been sure the Doctor was right behind her when she was running down the steps. He was after all remarkably light on his feet for a Time Lord. It was only when she stopped to draw a breath and turned to congratulate the Doctor on their successful escape that she discovered, with a sudden sickening shock, the Doctor was no longer with her. She was well and truly alone in Paradise Towers.

'Who are you?' The speaker was without doubt the leader of the uniformed attackers. A pompous, literal-minded, unintelligent sort of fellow, the Doctor decided very quickly. But then the Doctor was not going to feel well-disposed towards anybody whose minions had dragged him ignominiously from the spot at the bottom of the stairs where he had fallen, head over heels, in the attempt to escape.

'Well?'

The Doctor, brushing the dust from his coat and discovering to his relief that his umbrella was unharmed, decided to ignore the question. 'Are you the Caretakers?'

'Yes.' The middle-aged Caretaker looked very pleased with himself. He had a very high opinion of his position, all too apparently. The leader of the Caretakers perhaps, the Doctor wondered. Probably not, he decided. The man had all the signs of being a good, unquestioning second-in-command. No leader he. Still, after the threats and the arrows, there was something solid and comforting about the Caretakers. Their grey uniforms, tattered now, with soiled gold braiding and epaulettes half hanging off, must once have been rather smart. Nothing very military about them, of course. More like the sort of uniforms that the Doctor had seen on commissionaires outside smart London hotels on one of his visits to twentieth-century Earth. Maybe it was not such a bad thing to have been found by them.

'And you Caretakers take care? Of people too?' he enquired.

'Maybe.'

'Well,' the Doctor decided. 'You seem to be our safest bet

27

for the moment. Don't you think so, Mel?'

Mel was not there. Perhaps it was not very logical of the Doctor to expect her still to be there with him after all the frantic activity of the last few minutes but it did come as a surprise to realise she was nowhere in sight. He looked all about him but he could get no glimpse either of Mel or of a single Red Kang.

'Mel? Mel? Where are you?' The Doctor's voice rang out across the square but the only reply was a faint echo. 'I must find Mel.' The Doctor started to move off in the most likely direction, the direction he had been making for himself when they were still together.

'No, no, sunbeam,' the Caretaker snapped. 'You're coming with us.' The Doctor found himself lifted up almost bodily by two of the burlier Caretakers and pulled off in the opposite direction to the one he wanted to go.

'Mel! Mel!' The Doctor tried to glance back before he was dragged off on yet another enforced tour of Paradise Towers. Mel can take care of herself, he consoled himself. She won't come to any harm. I'll be able to give these fellows the slip before too long and we'll get together as arranged. It's a good thing that I made Mel make that agreement about meeting up at the pool.

Even Time Lords sometimes take credit for things they didn't think of themselves. The memory of the arrangement was enough to put him back in good spirits, anyway, as the Caretakers lead him away. It took him some time to remember that he had no idea what he was being led to.

28

3

Tea and Cakes

'Cooee! Would you care for a cup of tea?'

At first Mel thought she was hearing things. She was sitting dejectedly in a grimy ill-lit corridor in Paradise Towers and someone was offering her a cup of tea. It was so unlikely Mel thought her mind must be going.

'I said, would you care for a cup of tea?'

But no, there was the voice again. Mel looked along the corridor to where the voice appeared to be coming from. And, sure enough, standing there by an open door was a tiny, sweet-looking old lady. Her dress was somewhat bizarre, it was true, made up of bits and pieces of clothing in bright colours which didn't quite match, but she looked friendly and kind. And a cup of tea really would be very welcome.

'Thank you.' Mel got up, still rather dazed after her recent experiences, and moved towards the welcoming door. The old lady was carrying on a whispered conversation with someone inside and there were sounds of frenzied clearing-up. If Mel had been less tired, she might have wondered why the old lady prevented her from entering immediately. Over her hostess's shoulder, she did catch a glimpse of a capacious female figure disposing of the remnants of some meal or other. And her activity was followed by the whirr of something which sounded very much like a waste disposal unit. That was all.

'My friend, Tabby, is just tidying up,' explained the little old lady. 'We're both very house-proud, you see. Particularly when we have guests.' The whirring sounds inside stopped abruptly and the lady smiled encouragingly. 'I think it's all right to go in now.' She took Mel by the arm and led her over the threshold. 'I'm Tilda, by the way, what's your name?'

'Mel.'

'Mel,' repeated Tilda with relish. 'What a sweet name.' There was something about the way she said the words that didn't ring quite right even to Mel's tired ears. But the appeal of peace and quiet and tea was too strong for her.

The flat Mel was shown into was unlike anything she had yet seen in Paradise Towers. For a start, it was all sparkling clean and bright, with its cooker, its work surfaces and its waste disposal unit all gleaming white and its carpets free from stain or grime. And then there were the decorations. The flat was cluttered with them. Ducks on the wall. Huge garish flower vases. A glass topped table. Onyx ashtrays everywhere. There was even a bird cage with a budgerigar chirping away in it. The owners of the flat were undoubtedly great nestbuilders. Mel wondered how they could have survived amidst the squalor outside.

'Mel, this is Tabby.' Mel recognised the figure who had been scurrying about previously. Another old lady, dressed in a similar multi-coloured way, but this one was much larger, and, Mel couldn't help thinking, slightly more alarming. It was the front teeth, Mel decided, as she was introduced. They were unusually prominent, unusually strong-looking and very sharp. Rat's teeth, Mel thought, but then decided that was a very rude thing to think, especially as Tabby seemed every bit as friendly and welcoming as Tilda.

'Come in and make yourself comfortable.' the larger of the two ladies cooed, gesturing towards the shiny leatherette three-piece suite. And then she saw that Mel's hands were still tied. 'We can't allow that, can we, Tilda?'

'Certainly not,' Tilda concurred. 'Sit down, my dear, and let Tabby untie you. And I'll put the kettle on.' She skipped over to the kitchen section of the flat with surprising agility for one of her years.

'You must have been having a horrid time, you poor girl,' remarked Tabby while she was dexterously freeing the hands of the seated Mel. 'Who did this to you?'

'The Kangs,' Mel answered. 'The Red Kangs.'

'Tut, tut,' Tabby said, shaking her head. 'Those Kangs are naughty girls.' A suspicion suddenly entered her head. 'You're not a Kang, are you?'

Mel denied it hotly.

'We didn't think you were somehow,' Tilda put in as she bustled around getting the tea things ready. 'They're nasty, untrusting girls who would never take a cup of tea from harmless old folk like us, would they, Tabby?'

'No,' Tabby agreed, as she finished untying Mel. 'Mel's not at all like a Kang. She's a nice, polite, clean, well-spoken girl. Just the sort we like.'

'Excuse me –' Mel began, but before she could go on, Tabby had turned to Tilda and said, 'There you are, what did I say, lovely manners. Saying "Excuse me" before she asks a question.' Tabby turned back and fixed Mel with her large attentive eyes. 'What was it, dear?'

'I was going to ask who you were,' Mel explained.

'We're Tilda and Tabby, dear,' replied a puzzled Tilda. 'We've already told you.'

'No, no,' Mel persisted. 'I mean, like the Kangs are the Kangs and the Caretakers are the –'

The penny finally dropped. 'Oh, I see. Silly us,' Tabby giggled. 'We're the Rezzies. Short for Residents. Well, some of the Rezzies anyway. We've quite a few like-minded friends here and there in the Towers.'

Now she had taken in her surroundings and her strange hostesses, Mel was starting to wonder more about where they fitted in. 'Have you always lived here?'

'We've been here for ever such a long time if that's what you mean. How about you?'

'Oh, I'm just visiting,' Mel answered swiftly.

'A visitor?' Tabby's sharp eyes examined her wonderingly. 'Well, well, it must be a long time since the Towers saw any of those, eh, Tilda?'

'It takes you back, doesn't it?' sighed Tilda as she transferred some very odd-looking cakes onto doily-covered plates.

31

'Does it?' Mel's curiosity was returning by leaps and bounds now she was feeling more relaxed. 'What was it like before?'

'Never mind about that now,' Tilda chided. She brought over the tea things from the kitchen area and placed them on the glass-topped table in front of Mel. 'Have some tea and cakes.'

The cakes looked very rich and very fattening. They were also of shapes and colours that Mel had never seen before. But that didn't stop her mouth from watering. She realised how hungry she was feeling. Maybe questions could wait.

'You're a thin little thing, aren't you?' Tabby remarked, pushing a plate of the cakes towards her. 'Don't worry, dear, Tilda and I will feed you up.'

Mel selected a gooey confectionary monstrosity from the pile and bit into it. It tasted delicious. She would really have been very content if only she had been sure that the Doctor was safe. Tilda smiled as she tucked in. Tabby smiled too. Rat's teeth she thought again. And then forgot about it.

The Doctor meanwhile was being frog-marched through the corridors of the Towers at a tremendous pace by the over-zealous Caretakers. They had untied his hands but that was small consolation when he was being pulled along so fast that he was becoming quite breathless from the rush. He very quickly gathered that the leading Caretaker did everything by a well-thumbed rule book he carried in the inside pocket of his tattered uniform. The one word not found in this book was 'initiative'. The Caretaker would not have sneezed without checking on whether the rule book allowed it. And the Doctor's first impressions were confirmed from the scraps of conversation between his captors. This was no Chief Caretaker. This was the Deputy Chief Caretaker. The trusty right-hand man to somebody far cleverer and more powerful.

Every time the Doctor tried to stop and examine something, he was unceremoniously hauled away from it. It annoyed him having his natural curiosity frustrated and, as he became more and more breathless, he decided the time had come to put in for a rest.

'Surely the rules will allow us to slow down just for a moment,' he protested to the Deputy Chief. 'You may have been down this corridor hundreds of times but I haven't and I'd appreciate a moment to get my breath back and take in my surroundings. Will the rules run to that?'

But the inevitable rule book was already out of the Deputy Chief's pocket and he was thumbing through it laboriously. The Doctor waited impatiently. 'Well?'

'You're allowed to stop for one and a half minutes for every three thousand footsteps walked,' the Deputy Chief eventually concluded. 'That means you can stand still for a while.' The exact calculations for how long were clearly beyond him.

'Very generous of you,' the Doctor returned sarcastically. He took in the filthy and gloomy street in which they were standing. 'It must be a job keeping all these corridors clean and tidy.'

The irony was wasted on the Deputy Chief. 'Indeed,' he agreed. 'Especially the wallscrawl.' He indicated the brightly coloured paintings that covered every available wall space. The Doctor recognised the work of the Kangs. 'That's what you call them, isn't it? Wallscrawlers?'

The Deputy nodded. 'Dirty little pests.' He pointed to one wall in particular. And what the Doctor saw there quite took his breath away. The scrawl showed a girl dressed in yellow being threatened by two large white mechanical claws.

'It looks like a Kang and something attacking her. Some sort of machine? With a claw?' The Doctor knew instinctively that this was important.

'The Wallscrawlers make up a lot of silly pictures,' the Deputy put in swiftly, obviously hoping to close the conversation.

'Let's hope they are just silly pictures,' the Doctor returned, unconvinced. And then as he bent to examine the Kang wallscrawl more closely, the Doctor heard a sound, low at first, growing in volume. A soft mechanical whirring, regular but somehow menacing.

'What's that?' He turned questioningly to the Deputy.

'What's what?' The Deputy was suddenly very shifty, trying to pretend that there was no sound there at all. Then as the sound grew louder, he started to bluster. 'Look, sunshine, if there was anything wrong, there'd be instructions about how to deal with it in here, wouldn't there?'

But the Doctor was no longer paying attention. Down the corridor moving swiftly towards them was a large, gleaming white, wheeled robot, with headlights and blades swishing away at its sides. The Doctor was immediately fascinated as he was by all new encounters.

'Ah, I see,' he said, his eyes taking in the robot's contours. 'Some sort of robotic cleaner. With oltrimotive bi-curval scraping blades. Impressive workmanship.'

'You don't understand –' the Deputy Chief began, anxious now the Cleaner was approaching, to leave as soon as possible. Even his slow-moving brain sensed something was very wrong and he began to recall all the scaremongering that had been going the rounds of the Caretakers' Headquarters. But, unfortunately for him, his words had no effect on the Doctor who was heading straight towards the robotic cleaner.

'Now let's have a look at this oltrimotive blade, shall we?' the Doctor urged, edging closer and closer in his curiosity. The Deputy and the other Caretakers stood in a state of shock, unable either to help or hinder him. But they did see something the Doctor didn't. As he tried to look at the flashing steel blades protruding from its sides, the Cleaner had released from its top a large mechanical claw. Not unlike the one in the Wallscrawl. And menacing enough to suggest its purpose was not just to assist in picking up rubbish. The claw hovered threateningly above the Doctor's head ready to pounce as soon as the Cleaner was sufficiently close.

The Doctor's survival instincts were strong. Which was just as well. At almost the last moment he looked up and saw the claw reaching out towards him. He gave a gasp. The claw lunged towards him and he managed to evade its grasp and scamper off down the corridor to where the band of Caretakers stood transfixed.

'Do you do what I usually do in these circumstances?' the Doctor shouted as he ran towards them.

'What's that?' the Deputy Chief shouted back, galvanised into action by the sudden turn of events.

'Run!' called the Doctor. And run they all did as fast as they could. Prisoner and guards were suddenly all in the same boat. And the Cleaner with its menacing claw pursued them down the long deserted streets. There was much in this encounter that puzzled the Doctor. But there were times to sit and think. And times to run for your life.

'Quick, into the lift!' The Deputy Chief pointed to the end of the street where the lift door lay tantalisingly open and waiting. It was not far now but none of the runners had much energy left. While not that far behind them the Robotic Self-Activating Megapodic Mark 7Z Cleaner rolled relentlessly and speedily along in pursuit.

Somehow they all made it. Deputy, Doctor and Caretakers were packed sweating into the confined lift space. The Doctor looked at the control panel which informed them, correctly or not, that they were on the 23rd floor.

'I'm surprised any of the lifts in this place work,' he remarked.

'Most of them don't,' the Deputy replied, desperately pushing at the start button on the panel. Nothing happened. The doors didn't shut. The indicator still read Floor 23. And the Cleaner rolled along the street towards them with its claw at the ready.

The Deputy pushed the start button again, his rising panic barely under control. The doors remained obstinately open. The other Caretakers shifted uneasily. The Cleaner got closer.

'Here. Let me.' The Doctor decided it was time for action if they were not all to suffer the fate of the young girl in the wallscrawl. He for one had no intention of being clawed to death by a robot. He gathered all his strength and pushed. There was a pause. The Cleaner was nearly at the door now and flight was hopeless.

And then, in delayed response to the Doctor's efforts, the

doors slid shut. The Cleaner was excluded and the lift was in motion. The Doctor breathed a sigh of relief. The Caretakers were looking considerably more cheerful. And the lift was undoubtedly going upwards. Perhaps, the Doctor thought, towards some explanations for the bizarre happenings and extraordinary people he had experienced since entering Paradise Towers.

'I do hope Mel's all right,' he mused . . .

'Well, of course, in the old days, it was very different, wasn't it, Tabby?' The Rezzies were in full flood now that Mel was settled and tucking in to all the fattening fare they had laid before her.

'Very different,' Tabby agreed, spooning huge dollops of cream onto a green scone Mel was tackling. 'Lovely clean corridors. Nice fresh fountains. Airy lifts to go up and down the Towers whenever you wanted to.' She sighed. 'Even the Caretakers did their job properly in those days.'

'What happened then?' Mel was all attention.

'Difficult to say really.' Tabby spoke with a vagueness that may or may not have been deliberate. Mel found it hard to tell. 'My memory isn't what it was. But one thing followed another. And before we knew where we were, we were in the pickle we are today.'

Tilda looked wistful. 'Everybody has to fend for themselves, don't they, Tabby? Take what they can find.' And somehow or other, this thought led her to offer another sticky cake to an already well-filled Mel. From what they said the Rezzies could ill afford to be so generous but they were so persistent that Mel found it hard to say no without appearing to be rude. And with every mouthful she ate, she got the ridiculous idea that Tabby's big rat teeth were getting longer and sharper.

'So you were here from the beginning, were you?'

'Oh yes,' Tabby replied. 'From when the Great Architect finished Paradise Towers and all the youngsters and all the oldsters were brought here.'

'And the rest? The in-betweens?'

Tabby wrinkled her brow. 'I don't quite recall. But I think they had something else to do. A war to fight or something. It's all a very long time ago. I sometimes wonder whether we won that war or not, Tilda.'

Tilda shook her head sadly. 'I don't suppose we'll ever know.'

'Probably not.'

The Rezzies were silent and Mel saw an opportunity to ask something that she had been wanting to ask for some time. 'Do either of you know anything about a swimming pool?' She took a large bite of her sticky cake.

Again the Rezzies seemed unsure and again Mel could not decide whether the uncertainty was real or assumed. 'A swimming pool?' Tilda mused. 'No, I don't think so. Why do you want to know?'

'I have to meet someone there,' Mel returned, hoping they wouldn't ask her to be more specific. But the Rezzies seemed more concerned about the immediate situation. 'You'd be far better off forgetting about any pools and staying here with us, Mel, dear,' Tilda cooed. 'Wouldn't she, Tabby?'

'Oh yes, Tilda', Tabby agreed. 'She can eat and eat to her heart's content and get nice and plump and healthy. Safe from those nasty Kangs.'

Mel was beginning to find this kindness a bit oppressive. And she was beginning to worry about the Doctor. 'Look,' she explained, 'it's very kind of you but I'm afraid I will have to go once I've finished my tea. It's very important that I find out what's happened to my friend.'

'Oh nonsense, there's no rush,' Tilda urged. 'Finish your cake.'

Tabby's face burst into what was meant to be a reassuring smile but somehow the front teeth made it rather disturbing instead. 'We'll be very offended if you rush off so quickly, won't we, Tilda?' Tilda nodded energetically.

Mel felt herself weakening under the emotional blackmail. 'Well, just a few more minutes maybe,' she conceded.

'That's it, dear,' Tilda said contentedly. 'Plenty of time.'

'All the time in the world,' echoed Tabby. 'Make the most of the peace and quiet.'

37

And then the peace and quiet were suddenly shattered. There was a loud splintering sound and the flat's front door was smashed into innumerable pieces by a powerful unseen fist. All three women turned in surprise.

A large hole gaped now where the central wooden panel of the door had been. And through that hole stepped a man. Though not tall, he was an imposing figure with a rugged jaw, piercing eyes and a powerful, muscular body. He was the archetype of an action hero, Mel thought. The impression was increased by his commando-style outfit, the strange tattoo on his neck and the powerful-looking gun in his hand. He stood there just inside the door, rather too conscious of the impression of power and dynamism he was trying to create.

When he spoke it was to Mel and his voice was deep and strong. 'Are these old ladies annoying you?'

'No.' Now she had got over her surprise, Mel realised that she was rather annoyed with this intruder, with his assumption of his right to interfere in other people's business.

The intruder tried again. He pointed to Tabby and Tilda. 'Then are you annoying these old ladies?'

'No, she isn't,' Tilda snapped, even more annoyed than Mel. The stranger's confident pose was beginning to crumble under this lack of response. He was even starting to look somewhat crestfallen. The old ladies, who apparently knew him of old, pressed their advantage.

'I do wish you'd stop breaking through our door to try and save us,' Tabby exclaimed. 'We've had to repair it three times already. It's not as if we've ever been in any danger.'

'Except from bits of door flying all over the place,' added Tilda.

Mel's curiosity was roused. 'Look, who exactly are you?' she asked the newcomer.

He drew himself up and struck a pose that showed off how big his biceps were. The jaw was stuck out and the voice as self-consciously deep and authoritative as when he first came in. 'The name's Pex,' he announced proudly. 'I put the world of Paradise Towers to rights.'

And that, for the moment, was all Mel got out of him.

However, the excuse to leave now tea was interrupted was too good to miss and she started to say her goodbyes to Tabby and Tilda. They were very reluctant to let her go and Mel found herself once again finding their solicitude rather on the oppressive side.

'It does seem a pity when we were so comfortable,' Tilda kept saying.

'And you mustn't be put off by him,' Tabby added, with a withering glance at Pex who remained stuck in his heroic pose blocking the way out.

Mel glanced at him and decided that Pex wasn't really alarming at all. He was actually a bit ridiculous. 'Don't worry about that,' she assured the Rezzies. 'But I do have to find my friend – and the pool.'

'You will come back and see us though, won't you?' Tilda urged.

'Maybe bring your friend,' Tabby put in with a gleam in her eye Mel didn't quite understand.

'Of course, I will,' she assured them. 'And thank you for everything.'

And she stepped through the hole in the front door Pex had created, feeling oddly rather relieved to be away from these kind old ladies. However, she was not to feel relieved and alone for very long. As they came to wave goodbye to Mel, the Rezzies very firmly ordered Pex from their flat. And now as she made her way back down the street, Mel became aware that she was being followed.

'Just a moment,' Pex was calling.

Mel turned to face him, liking him no more than before. 'What is it now?'

'You are going on a difficult journey,' he announced smugly, striking another pose designed to show off his muscular development. 'You need me to protect you.'

'I most certainly do not.'

'But that's my job. I am Pex. I put the world of Paradise Towers to rights.'

39

Pex's conceit seemed to be immeasurable and Mel found herself especially annoyed by the assumption that she wasn't able to manage on her own without this lumbering male tagging along. She said as much and, again, Pex started to wilt under her indignation. It was only when she caught a glimpse of this vulnerability that she found she could like him a little more. Perhaps sensing this, Pex tried again to persuade her to take him along. There was something almost plaintive in his tone now and Mel began to realise that in some odd way it was very important to him that she accepted him.

'If you don't need a protector then you might need a guide. Somebody who knows their way about.'

He had a point. Paradise Towers was a vast baffling building and Mel hadn't begun to work out how it was planned. 'All right,' she agreed, 'you've got the job.'

She walked off down the street and Pex, happier now she had accepted him, followed on just behind. It was true that a guide would be helpful in tracing the Doctor and that Pex must know the ill-lit and confusing streets a lot better than she did. All the same, Mel couldn't help wondering whether she might live to regret letting this self-appointed protector tag along.

4

The Chief

Somehow the Chief Caretaker had the feeling that all was not exactly as it should be. And for somebody as methodical in his ways as the Chief Caretaker it was not a very comfortable feeling to have.

Normally it gave him a nice, snug glow of satisfaction to sit there in his Headquarters surrounded by screens that told him what was going on in every single corner of Paradise Towers. Everything ran according to the rules in the rule book and none of the Caretakers ever questioned anything. Not even who had first invented all the rules in the rule book. The only thorn in his flesh was the Wallscrawlers and, though they were sometimes a nuisance, he could usually keep them in order with the odd surprise raid like the one he had ordered that morning on Fountain of Happiness Square. All in all, life in Paradise Towers seemed to run on the well-oiled lines that he had laid down for it and all was well with the world.

Not, of course, that even a Chief Caretaker didn't need a spot of relaxation. For that he had adopted a pet in the Basement of the Towers whom he visited now and then. The Chief Caretaker couldn't really remember quite how contact had first been made but now he spent a great deal of his waking life thinking about how best to serve his pet. Pets often have good appetites and this particular pet had a mountainous appetite which the Chief Caretaker did his best to satisfy. After all, like any proud owner, he wanted his pet to grow up big and strong. A particularly satisfying part of the morning had been spent in despatching to the Basement in a Robotic Self-activating Megapodic Mark 7Z Cleaner the remains of

the now defunct Caretaker number 345 stroke 12 subsection 3.
The Chief had watched the Cleaner carrying its load on one of
his screens and thought what a tasty little snack Caretaker
number 345 stroke 12 subsection 3 would be for his pet. Even
tastier than the Yellow Kang he had despatched earlier.
Somehow moments like that gave the extra satisfaction that
made his demanding job really worthwhile.

So where had his feeling of unease come from? That was the
question and he didn't really have an answer. Perhaps even he
could not really believe that a world as well-regulated as
Paradise Towers, a world so well tailored to his own personal
convenience, could stay exactly that way for ever. Perhaps it
was not given to a man to have a powerful, rewarding job,
obedient subordinates and a lovely secret pet to care for. He
had no positive evidence to fuel his anxieties.

The Chief sat staring at his screens. In one a Caretaker
moved down Nitrate Street removing Wallscrawl. In another
two Rezzies scuttled past on their way home. On a third a lift,
which had been jammed on Floor 207 for as long as anyone
could remember, stayed jammed on Floor 207. On several
screens the Chief's beloved Cleaners went about their work.
Cleaning, that was. The Cleaners' special services were only
occasionally called on and with great discretion. The other
Caretakers must not be upset . . .

The Chief was a man of middle height dressed in a once
grand, grey uniform and cap, decorated with braid and
insignia, now somewhat faded and dusty. The Chief was not a
vain man and there were more important things than sartorial
elegance. His sallow complexion and drooping black
moustache showed signs of neglect too. The Chief was not
keen on fresh air or healthy exercise. He regarded such
activities as futile, even actively harmful.

As his bloodshot but alert eyes scanned the screens, the
Chief began to feel calmer. Everything was proceeding just as
normal. What had he got to worry about?

And then the screen that covered the approach to the
Headquarters itself flickered into life. That meant someone

42

was approaching. The Deputy, of course, returning from his raid on Fountain of Happiness Square. The Chief Caretaker leant forward to see more clearly whether the Deputy /had taken any Kangs prisoners. Kangs, after all, were tasty snacks for the Chief's pet. Smaller than Caretakers but less fatty.

There was a figure with the Deputy. The Chief could see that much. But it wasn't a Kang or a Rezzie. It was a man, oddly attired, carrying an umbrella. A sudden tremor went through the Chief as the man came more clearly into view.

It wasn't possible. It couldn't be.

He passed a hand over his brow thoughtfully. It could be.

The journey in the lift had not been a pleasant experience for the Doctor. There was barely room to breathe, clamped between the sweating and obese Caretakers. And the lift itself juddered so much that he expected it to stop completely at any moment. All in all, he was extremely relieved to be out of it and walking down another street, however ill-lit and dirty, on what was obviously the final leg of his journey with the Deputy.

They arrived at a very solid-looking metal door. The Deputy produced a small square from his pocket and inserted it in a tiny slot so well concealed that the Doctor would never have noticed it of its own accord.

The door slid open and the Doctor was bundled inside. Soon he was in a large room whose walls were covered in screens relaying pictures from every part of the Towers. The multiplying and constantly changing images were dazzling at first.

A figure seated studying these screens turned as the Doctor was hustled in by the Deputy, who was full of the importance of the occasion. The figure rose and the Doctor came face to face with a man whose very presence breathed an air of authority for all the seediness of his appearance.

The Deputy's self-important explanations were brushed aside. The Doctor's release was ordered and the Caretakers took a step back leaving their leader confronting the Doctor with an odd, unexplained gleam in his eye.

'Greetings,' the Doctor began, simply in order to break the silence.

'Greetings,' the other man's face cracked into a less than pleasant smile. 'I am the Chief Caretaker.

'And I am –' the Doctor began. But he didn't get any further in his introduction. To his surprise he found his speech cut off by the Chief Caretaker exclaiming enthusiastically, 'No need to tell me. I know who you are.'

The Doctor stared. He had not realised his name was already known here. But before he could ask more, the Chief was off again, an enthusiastic torrent of words, addressed as much to the waiting Caretakers as to the Doctor himself.

'Oh yes, we have been waiting for this momentous visit for so many years,' he began, his bloodshot eyes lighting up with enthusiasm. He patted the Doctor warmly on the back. 'You are the man who brought Paradise Towers to life. The visionary who dreamed up its pools and lifts and squares. And now you have returned to your creation.'

He pressed his face closer to the Doctor's, eyes agleam. 'You will make all those dilapidated lifts rise and fall as they have never done before. All signs of wallscrawl will disappear from the corridors of Paradise Towers. The floors will gleam. The fountains will tinkle. The windows will shine. The grass will grow. And all will be made as new.'

The Doctor was so mesmerised by the ardour of this speech that he found it impossible to interrupt it. But there was an obvious misapprehension here and he had better put it right before things got out of hand. He didn't want to start on the wrong foot. Now seemed the appropriate moment and he opened his mouth to speak.

But the Chief, oblivious of this, had now turned to the attendant Caretakers. 'Fellow Caretakers,' he exclaimed, 'do you know who this is?' Their silence showed all too clearly that they didn't. 'This is the Great Architect returned to Paradise Towers. Bid him welcome. All hail the Great Architect! All hail!'

44

The Great Architect! Now the Doctor understood what the mistake was. It was crucial that as soon as possible he explained that he was not the Architect responsible for the Towers. Before they asked him to make the lifts work or clean out the fountains. Again, he tried to speak.

'All hail! All hail the Great Architect!'

The Caretakers had all taken up the Chief's cry now, completely drowning out the Doctor's explanations. Obedient to their Chief as ever, the Caretakers were putting their hearts into it and considering what an unfit, ill-matched and shambolic bunch they really were, the effect was remarkably stirring. What a pity, the Doctor thought, they've got hold of the wrong end of the stick.

'What shall we do with him now then, Chief?' The cheering had subsided and the Deputy Chief had stepped forward deferentially to receive the Chief's orders.

There was a brief pause while the Chief examined the Doctor with the same disturbing gleam in his eye and a smile on his lips. He patted the Doctor on the back amicably and then gave the order, short, sharp and savage.

'Kill him!'

The contrast was so startling that the Doctor could scarcely believe his ears. The misunderstanding had gone far enough.

'Just a moment,' he protested as loudly as he could. 'Listen.'

'Why?' There was silence now and the Chief was icy cool.

'I'm not the Great Architect. I'm the Doctor.' Surely the Chief wasn't going to persist in this charade, the Doctor assured himself.

But he was. Now he was turning to the Caretakers and bringing them into the debate. 'He was always very artful, the Great Architect,' he explained, almost as an aside. And then as casually as he had beckoned to the Deputy. 'Make the preparations will you?'

'Yes Chief.' There was no point in trying to convince the Deputy that there had been a mistake. He waited for further instructions from his boss.

'The 327 Appendix Subsection 9 Death, I think,' the Chief

announced judiciously, after some thought.

'Very good, Chief.' The Deputy was half way across the room to grab hold of the Doctor again when a loud bleeping sound started up. It was coming from the elaborate control panel that stretched across one wall beneath the screens. When he heard it, the Deputy stopped. It was the first hopeful sound the Doctor had heard since entering the Caretakers' Headquarters.

'It would happen just now.' With a weary sigh, the Chief flicked up a switch on the panel and listened attentively to the voice at the other end, inaudible to all but him. His face assumed a concerned air though the Doctor, more observant in such cases than the Caretakers, strongly suspected the concern was less than sincere.

'Oh dear, oh dear,' the Chief kept on exclaiming intermittently as the distant voice babbled on. 'Poor Caretaker number 345, stroke 12, subsection 3.' He listened some more. 'You want me to come now? But I'm in the middle of something rather important.' The voice became agitated and the Chief more testy. 'All right, all right,' he conceded eventually, 'there's no need to quote the rule book at me, Caretaker number 569, stroke 14, subsection 8. I'll come.'

He flicked the switch back up again and turned pensively back to the waiting room, all too obviously irritated by the interruption.

'Anything the matter?' the Doctor enquired innocently.

'Nothing that isn't under control, thank you, Great Architect,' was the tart reply. The Chief called the Deputy over and again there was that look of concern in his face that the Doctor did not quite believe. The Deputy Chief, however, obviously did.

'An unfortunate accident has occurred to Caretaker number 345 stroke 12 subsection 3,' the Chief announced gravely. 'I am required by the rulebook to go and investigate it. The 327 Appendix 3 Subsection 9 Death will be postponed until I return. In the meantime, you will guard the Great Architect here with your lives. Understand?'

'Yes Chief,' the Deputy nodded. 'No problem.'

A few moments later and the Chief Caretaker was gone. The threat of the 327 Apendix 3 Subsection 9 Death, however, had not. So thought the Doctor as he was led away to a bench and seated on it between the Deputy and one of the biggest and burliest of the other Caretakers. He had only his brain power to rely on to help him out of this sticky situation. If the Chief had remained, he would not have fancied his chances one bit. But sandwiched between two large but not remarkably intelligent dogsbodies of the Chief there might just be a chance. He certainly hoped so.

'Hail the Kang. Hail the unalive Kang. Yellow of colour but brave and bold as a Kang should be.'

The words of the lone Blue Kang were taken up and repeated by the others.

'Hail the Kang . . . Yellow of Colour but brave and bold as a Kang should be . . . Brave and bold as a Kang should be . . .'

Mel watched fascinated. In a corner of one of the squares of Paradise Towers, a structure of metal scrap had been built, improvised, no doubt, by scouring through the rubbish that littered the surrounding corridors. The Blue Kangs were circling it now, their eerie words building into a chant. From where she was concealed, Mel had difficulty in making out what they were saying. She strained her ears.

'Yellow of colour but brave and bold as a Kang should be . . .'

And then she noticed right on top of the pile of scrap, so carefully and lovingly assembled, a yellow banner. Bloodstained, she thought. Was this a ceremony then for a Yellow Kang? The Red Kangs had told Mel and the Doctor that they were all 'unalive' so was this some sort of funeral celebration? It was the only explanation that made sense.

She could have asked Pex, who was by her side, also flattened against the wall to evade detection. But she had already begun to suspect that her own common sense would tell her as much as he could. His attempts to guide her through the streets of the Towers had not been encouraging. They had already negotiated several dead ends and come across the same fountain in the same square four times. At least they were now in a different square. And the Blue Kangs' ceremony had a seriousness and even sadness that was impressive. They seemed so young to have such a grasp of the need for mourning and ritual.

They were laying their metal crossbows around the Yellow Kang's funeral shrine now as a gesture of respect. The chanting continued.

'Brave and bold . . .'

Pex coughed nervously. He had a point. They shouldn't stay here too long. Discovery would almost certainly lead to another arrest and there was no guarantee that she would be as lucky in evading the Blue Kangs as she had been with the Reds. Besides, she had to find the Doctor.

Stealthily she crept away. Inevitably Pex followed. The chanting faded as they moved off down one of the streets that led off the square. Mel had chosen it at random but she didn't feel she could do any worse in this than by following Pex's examples.

They soon came to a new street, rather brighter and cleaner than most. An unusually ornate type of streetlamp jutted from its walls, spreading a softer, warmer light. Mel started to feel more relaxed. The ceremony had brought home to her how common death seemed to be in the Towers and the words of the Blue Kang chant had lodged in her brain. She was glad to be in a more cheerful environment.

Unfortunately the ornate lamps with their wrought-iron holders gave Pex a new confidence as well. He had been quite subdued when they were in the Square but now he stopped and called on Mel to stop too. Reluctantly Mel turned. From the complacent expression on Pex's face, she strongly suspected that he was about to give her a demonstration of his talents. She had already been delayed by several exhibitions of prowess and she was in no mood for another. She had just got to hope it wouldn't waste too much time.

'Mel – watch this!' Pex sensed her impatience and added. 'It

48

won't take a moment.' But, of course, it did. First there were the physical preparations. Much flexing of arm muscles and rhythmic deep breathing. Then there was a long pause while Pex simply grasped the streetlamp he had selected and stood there gathering his concentration. And then there was the strenuous effort as he snapped the holder off from the wall. And then there was even more strenuous and protracted effort of bending and twisting the lamp with his bare hands. And finally the triumphant throwing down of the stout, once-elegant fitment now turned into a fantastic corkscrew of twisted metal.

Once it was all over Pex assumed an air of casual nonchalance as if it had cost him no effort at all.

'Well?' Mel had watched this display with increasing impatience at its futility.

'You have to be strong to do that,' Pex protested. 'And fit. And trained. There aren't many people who could do that.'

'I can't think of many who'd want to,' Mel returned tartly.

'But, Mel,' Pex continued indignantly, 'you don't realise. I'm a finely tuned fighting machine. I work out every day. Practise martial arts. Run the length of seventeen carrydoors each morning. I –'

'Pex –' Mel cut in, unable to contain herself any longer. 'If you could bend that back into shape and put it back where it came from, that might be more useful. But you can't, can you?'

'That's not my job. I'm Pex and –'

Mel had heard this refrain countless times already. 'I know, you're Pex and "you're here to put the world of Paradise Towers to rights". Well, go ahead. I've got to find my friend. And I can't waste any more time.'

She walked off down the street but Pex was soon following after her. His persistence made her decide to be brutally frank. As he caught up again, she found herself getting very angry.

'Just tell me one thing, Pex,' she began, 'if you're so marvellous, why doesn't anybody else in Paradise Towers want your help? I should have thought there are plenty of wrongs to put right here without bothering me. Or is everybody else so fed up with you knocking down their doors

49

and smashing their street lights that they don't want to have anything to do with you?'

Her anger had made her go too far. Pex's square-jawed face had started to crumple. She had guessed correctly. Pex was an outcast. She should have guessed that from the contempt with which the Rezzies had treated him. But the realisation actually made her position more difficult. If he had simply been brutal and stupid, she could have ditched him with an easy heart. But instead, despite her exasperation, she kept feeling sorry for him. And that was fatal for her plans of going it alone.

'Shall I tell you what puzzles me most?' The Doctor asked the question brightly but knew there would be no reply.

The Deputy on his right and the burly Caretaker on his left sat there stolidly and impassively, repeatedly refusing to rise to the bait. The Doctor, however, persisted. Perhaps, sooner or later, he would touch the right chord and one or other of his jailers would open up. Besides, he wanted very much to get to the bottom of what was going on even if he was to suffer a 327 Appendix 3 Subsection 9 Death afterwards.

'It's those robotic cleaners we had such a nasty time with,' he continued, answering his own question. 'Presumably they're part of the organisation of Paradise Towers like you Caretakers. They clean it up and you look after law and order. So why did they attack you?'

Another question met with stony silence. 'And another thing,' he persisted, 'I don't understand why you're all so keen to kill off the Great Architect. I'd've thought you'd be delighted to have him here to put Paradise Towers back in good repair. It's peculiar, isn't it?'

The Deputy Chief's only reply was to shift slightly on the bench. The Doctor decided he had to try another tack. He assumed a pitying expression. 'I'd hate to have to live my whole life by some boring old rule book as you do. You must get very bored.' He paused. 'Well, do you?'

'No.' Not much of a speech, the Doctor thought, but it was a start.

'Never?'

'Never.'

Two replies to questions in a row. The Doctor was beginning to have the germ of an idea, which, with luck on his side, might just work. He decided to follow this more fruitful vein of conversation. 'I suppose how you guard me is in the rule book too?'

'Yes,' the Deputy could not resist replying, 'Regulation 47b subsection 2.'

'You know,' the Doctor began, casually, 'I'd be most interested in taking a look at that rule book. If it's not against the rules.' The Deputy pursed his lips. 'After all I am a condemned man.'

A lengthy examination of certain sections of the well-thumbed rule book now ensued. To the Doctor, it seemed interminable. But he knew the Deputy Chief would do nothing without the rule book and he had to be patient. Finally, the Deputy looked up with grim satisfaction and announced, 'We'll count it as your last request. You're entitled to one if you're going to undergo a 327 Appendix 3 Subsection 9 Death.' He smirked as he ceremoniously handed the book over. 'It's not a pretty way to go.'

The Doctor took the rule book eagerly. He started to flick through the pages, crammed with tiny printed columns of rules and regulations to cover every conceivable eventuality from AIR INTAKE to ZYGOPHYTES, but his mind was already racing on to the next stage of his plan. He selected a page at random – it seemed to concern mainly WINDOW-CLEANING – and studied it with apparent rapt attention. After a few minutes, he exclaimed in amazed tones, 'How extraordinary. It can't be true.' The Deputy Chief was all attention at once but the Doctor pretended not to notice. 'No, no, it's so unlikely, you couldn't possibly –' he continued, shaking his head.

The Deputy Chief was nettled by the implied criticism. 'If it's there then it's true. Rules are rules and orders are orders.'

'If you say so,' the Doctor returned, shaking his head, 'I

don't want to make a fool of you.'

'Just read out what it says.'

Here was the crux of the Doctor's gamble. He just had to hope that even the Deputy Chief could not memorise the entire contents of such a tome. But by now the Deputy was so angry with the Doctor for daring to question the book by which he ordered his entire life that the Doctor could not put off the attempt any longer.

'Well, he began slowly, taking a surreptitious glance at his watch in preparation, 'according to what I've just read here, it seems that after you've been guarding your condemned prisoner for thirty-five minutes, you must all stand up.'

'But –' The Deputy was puzzled but did not appear to doubt the authenticity of what he heard. Nor notice the coincidence of the time period specified being exactly the same as had elapsed since the Chief had left.

'I know it sounds silly,' the Doctor agreed sympathetically, 'and of course, I'm not expecting you to do it. But it is in the rule book.'

The Doctor got to his feet. The Deputy Chief hesitated for a moment. And then to the Doctor's intense relief, he rose too, and the other Caretakers with him. Rules, after all, were rules.

Pushing his advantage, the Doctor continued. 'The Caretakers present must then move five paces away from the prisoner . . .' The Caretakers did this unhesitatingly, the Doctor noted happily. Now for it.

'Close their eyes and put their hands above their heads . . .'

Just when he thought they were bound to smell a rat, the Caretakers obeyed. Eyes closed, hands on heads, five paces away. It was time now to carefully put down the rule book on the bench and tiptoe stealthily towards the Deputy. He had noted on their first arrival where the Deputy kept the small square he used to unlock the door of the Headquarters. In his back pocket. It would be a matter of moments to pull it out.

'How long does the book say we do this?' Eyes still closed, the Deputy was starting to get impatient. But even as he spoke, the Doctor's nimble fingers had found the small square and were in the process of drawing it out of his pocket. Just a little more time needed.

'Oh, about a minute and a half,' the Doctor improvised, the key-card now firmly in his hand. He was already on his way to the exit door. 'That's how long the prisoner needs . . .'

'Needs? To do what?'

The Doctor had found where the key-square should be inserted and was pushing the card into place. The door slid silently open. 'To find the key-card to the door and escape,' he explained cheekily.

'Sorry?'

'To find the key-card to the door and escape.' The Doctor was through the door now and it was starting to close again. The Deputy would surely be opening his eyes any second now.

'But that doesn't make sense. Why should we –'

But the door was shut now and the rest of the Deputy Chief's sentence was cut off from the Doctor's ears. He was outside the Headquarters again and with a short start on his jailors. There was no time to lose. He started to run back the only way he knew, the way he had come. Somehow, he didn't want to stay around to hear the rest of the Deputy's comments. Or the Chief's, for that matter.

Bin Liner was waiting anxiously. The Red Kangs were re-assembling after the Caretakers' attack at the pre-arranged spot on Floor 12 close to talkiphone 4. But they were not all there yet. She could not stand the thought that more Red Kangs might be unalive.

Finally Fire Escape arrived. 'Build High for Happiness.'

'Build High for Happiness.'

The two leaders exchanged the Kang salute. But Fire Escape saw Bin Liner's unease.

'All sound and safe?'

'The unyoung Doctor and the girl who is no Kang are lost for now.'

Fire Escape shrugged. It was not a great loss. But she

53

looked anxiously about the assembled familiar faces and failed to find one of them. 'Where is No Exit?'

'Was on talkiphone 3 before the Caretakers' attack . . .' Bin Liner's voice trailed away.

'Not now?' Fire Escape pressed.

But all Bin Liner could do was shake her head glumly.

'Mayhaps No Exit's returned to Red Kang Brainquarters,' Fire Escape argued but without much conviction. Both of them instinctively knew that the chances were that No Exit, their companion since childhood, a redder than red Kang, was unalive. They were used to loss but it still hurt them every time.

All Kangs knew what happened to the unalive. They were taken to the Cleaners. It was not part of the Kang game but still it happened. What they didn't know, what no-one knew, not even the Chief Caretaker, complacently providing little snacks for his pet, was what was happening in the Basement of Paradise Towers. No Exit was taken to the Cleaners but where would the Cleaners take her after that?

The Red Kangs went back to their Brainquarters dejectedly, an isolated and dejected piece of the puzzle that was Paradise Towers.

5

This Way and That

Mel felt she should be getting better at knowing her way round Paradise Towers by now but it didn't seem to be turning out that way. So many corridors looked the same. So many broken-down lifts with control panels giving totally contradictory indications as to what floor they were on. So many grimy, indistinguishable, winding staircases to be climbed between floors. It was hard not to get depressed. And harder still to believe that she would ever find the Doctor. They could pass so close to each other in this concrete jungle, one going up, one going down, one going left, one going right, without even knowing. It was only the distant hope that they would both be able, by some means or other, to make it to the swimming pool that sustained her.

And then that hope almost faded. After seemingly hours of trying to work their way up the building, they were back at Fountain of Happiness Square. Right where they started. Mel realised she should have known better than to leave any of the decisions about which turning to take to Pex. She was certainly paying the price now.

'I've been trying to confuse anybody who might be following,' Pex explained lamely as they dispiritedly scanned the all-too-familiar square. 'It's part of my training.'

'Does your training include confusing yourself at the same time?' Mel couldn't help enquiring.

'I'm not confused,' Pex returned defensively.

'So you do know how to get us up to the pool then, do you?'

'Of course.'

'Well then?'

There was no reply. Pex looked around hopelessly at all the ways that led from the square. Mel was not surprised, of course, but she was tired and she had had enough. 'Pex,' she began, 'can I ask you something?'

'What?'

'Why are you here?'

Pex stared.

'I mean, there's no one else like you here, is there?' Pex looked quite flattered by this remark and struck a heroic pose but Mel persisted. 'Tabby and Tilda talked about a war. They said only the oldsters and the youngsters were brought to Paradise Towers and the rest – the in-betweens – were sent off to fight and never came back. So how does it happen that you're here?'

Pex was defiant. 'Isn't it obvious?'

'No,' Mel countered, 'it isn't obvious at all. Pex, you say you want to help me get up to the pool and find my friend, the Doctor, so I have to know.'

Pex was thoughtful. 'I was sent here,' he announced. 'The power to protect has been invested in me.'

The words were powerful and impressive and Pex's conviction as he spoke them made Mel almost believe him. Maybe he had been sent. Anything was possible in a set-up as crazy as Paradise Towers. 'Who by, Pex?'

'By those who i am not allowed to name.' Pex's tone was mysterious now, hinting at forces behind Mel's comprehension. She was still uncertain.

'And that's the truth, Pex? Really the truth?' He nodded solemnly. Mel knew that she had no real choice but to believe him. There was certainly no time to waste arguing. They had been hanging around in the square too long for comfort already.

'You're in no danger with me around,' Pex assured her. Her trust in him seemed to give him new strength and he started to walk across the square towards the one way out of the square they hadn't tried. Mel followed.

As did two Blue Kangs who had overheard every word that had been said.

*

'Now the main thing, fellow Caretakers, is not to panic –'

The Chief was into his stride now, pacing up and down the section of Potassium Street where the young Caretaker had met his fate. A group of frightened Caretakers listened attentively, one of them clutching the deceased's standard issue QY6 cap, stained now, unfortunately, with non-standard issue blood.

'Just because it appears that something unfortunate may have happened to Caretaker number 345 stroke 12 subsection 3, we must not go leaping to conclusions.' The Chief's eyes scanned his attentive subordinates. 'Careless chat about the Robotic Self-Activating Megapodic Mark 7Z Cleaners having got out of control is not going to help anyone and may needlessly upset other Caretakers.'

The assembled Caretakers shifted uneasily. Conversations on the subject were commonplace back in the HQ and they all secretly hoped that the Chief would not guess how many of them had been involved in so-called careless chat.

'Everything in the whole of Paradise Towers is perfectly in order as always and running exactly according to the rules set down in the rule book,' the Chief insisted grandly. 'You will ignore any evidence to the contrary.'

Internally, however, he wondered if the same unease that he had felt might be shared by his docile crew. If it was, he must act quickly to stifle discontent. 'You may rest assured that I will undertake a thorough investigation of what has happened and prepare a full and detailed report as demanded by Emergency Regulation 9P2.' He paused. 'In the meantime, all Caretakers will patrol their assigned streets as before. I am sure you will be quite safe.'

If there was going to be a protest of any sort, this was when it would be made, the Chief thought. But the Caretakers, though looking unhappy, said nothing.

Then there was a bleep on the Chief's Mark 12 Long Distance Communication Expediter. It was the Deputy Chief. And the report he had to make was one he knew the Chief did not wish to hear. The prisoner had escaped, the Deputy explained in embarrassed and fearful tones.

The Chief spoke for the benefit of the assembled Caretakers as well as the distant and quaking Deputy Chief. His voice was menacing. 'Find him,' he ordered. 'Find the Great Architect at once.' He paused grimly. 'I don't think I need to remind anyone just how unpleasant a 327 Appendix 3 Subsection 9 death can be.'

The Doctor sighed with relief. He was fairly certain he had lost the pursuing Caretakers. And so, finally, after frantically rushing down flights of rubbish-strewn stairs and along sordid streets, he could pause to mop his brow. When he had his breath back, he would find a way of getting to the pool – and Mel.

As soon as he started to take in his surroundings, he became aware of the quantity of Kang wallscrawl there was about. And one drawing in particular took his notice. It showed a Kang threatened by a Cleaner, its claw reaching out towards the girl in a way that the Doctor found uncomfortably familiar. But this time the Cleaner had some sort of cart in tow behind it. And out of the cart were sticking legs, the legs presumably of earlier victims. A cart? To take the bodies where? The next scrawl showed some sort of door with smoke belching out of it. What was being burnt behind that door? The drawings raised as many questions as they answered but were certainly worth recording. The Doctor started to trace a copy of the wallscrawl into his pocket book, with the intention of studying them more fully later.

The approach of a Cleaner was very quiet and smooth. The Doctor ought to have known that by now but once again he was taken by surprise. The Cleaner was almost upon him before he looked up from his drawing. The Doctor was not alarmed this time, merely peeved. He had a lot to do and the robot needn't think it was going to fool him with its oltrimotive bi-curval scraping blades.

'You don't catch *me* the same way twice,' he informed the Megapodic Cleaner as it neared him. 'I know what you're going to do next.'

He waited smugly for the familiar claw to appear. It didn't. Instead the Cleaner started to spray from its front an evil-smelling smoke. Its taste was acrid. The effect practically lethal. The Doctor started to choke and splutter. He had to move or he would suffocate. No doubt of that. He turned and started to run as fast as his wheezing lungs would allow him. Pride comes before a fall, the Doctor told himself. Will I never learn?

The Cleaner followed, billowing its noxious smoke as it went. The Doctor had gained some ground by the time he turned into the next street. But not enough. He would tire and the Cleaner would not.

He started to look round for some aid in his plight. And his eye caught a metal notice nailed to one of the walls. 'For Emergencies' it read. That was surprising enough. But, even more surprising, underneath the notice was what looked remarkably like an emergency telephone.

'Nothing ventured,' the Doctor told himself, running to the phone. He picked up the receiver, but , of course, the phone was dead. He realised he should have known better than to expect anything to work in Paradise Towers. And so, with the Cleaner approaching nearer by the moment, it was also nothing gained.

He sighed and slumped back against the wall to recover his breath before continuing his frantic flight. In leaning back, he must somehow or other have touched a button or gadget on the side of the phone. For, suddenly, without warning, coin tokens started pouring out of the machine. They poured in a clatter onto the floor, hundreds of them, and lay there gleaming amidst the garbage.

The Doctor stooped and picked up some of them. They were all identical, shiny and embossed. And all carried the same inscription. The Doctor brought one even closer to see what it said. 'Issued by the Great Architect, Kroagnon' ran the inscription.

Kroagnon. The name rang a bell but infuriatingly the Doctor couldn't remember why. There were so many puzzles and he desperately needed time to think. But how he was going to get even a minute to think with a Cleaner spraying noxious fumes in pursuit was an even bigger puzzle. It was so infuriating not to have time even to place a name.

'You really aren't helping, you know,' he called out angrily down the street to the Cleaner. 'What do you want anyway?'

And then, from behind him, he thought he heard the soft mechanical whirring of a different machine. He glanced over his back. Yes, another Cleaner was coming towards him from the other direction, spraying smoke as it came. He was trapped between them and, if there had been any doubt, it was now absolutely clear what the Cleaners wanted. His death.

'Think calmly.' The smoke was billowing around him and the Cleaners were practically upon him. Smoke, claws, blades. It soon wouldn't matter which way they chose to dispose of him.

His hands scrabbled blindly along the wall by the telephone. His coughing was violent now and his breathing irregular and painful. Something told him there was a door there. A door perhaps just to a cupboard but still a door. His fingertips could trace part of its outline. If only there was some way of opening it.

The Cleaners closed for the kill. And the Doctor's hand with its last ounce of strength found a tiny lever hidden in the wall. The door sprang open and the Doctor felt himself catapulted away from the Cleaners, away from the smoke, down, down into blackness. He heard the door snapping shut behind him. It was the last sound he remembered before the blackness swallowed him.

Mel and Pex were on the twelfth floor now, if the signs were to be believed and they probably weren't. But the lift ahead looked the best maintained Mel had seen yet. Perhaps this might be the one, the miraculous lift in Paradise Towers that actually worked properly. It was worth a try anyway.

She started towards the lift but Pex restrained her. 'Wait there. I'll check if it's safe.'

Mel started to say that she was perfectly capable of doing her own checking but he had bounded to the entrance to the lift before she could get the words out.

'Well?'

'It's safe.' Pex beckoned her to approach. But, as he beckoned, two Blue Kangs stepped from the shadows beside the lift, crossbows at the ready. Mel turned to run. But her escape route was blocked by more Blue Kangs, crossbows also at the ready. They must have been following Pex and herself for some time. She gritted her teeth. Thank you for checking so well, Pex, she thought.

There must have been five or six of them in all, gathered in an ominous circle around their prisoners. Now she could see them closely, Mel could see that in all but colour they closely resembled the Red Kangs. Even the weapons were similar. And no doubt equally accurate.

'Come on, come on.' Pex had suddenly struck an extraordinary martial pose. It reminded Mel of the karate experts she had watched back on Earth but the pose was both more extravagant and more blatantly aggressive. With his jaw jutting out and his powerful arms poised, Pex was an impressive sight.

To Mel at least. The Blue Kangs watched impassively as Pex ranted at them. 'I'll take you all on,' he announced, shooting out a tautened arm. 'Look, with my bare hands I'll do it.' To Mel's surprise he almost managed a snarl. 'I'm a trained fighting machine. Come on. Fight . . . Fight . . .'

None of the Kangs rose to the challenge. They just watched and under their gaze Pex's gestures became less confident.

'Enough, Musclebrain, get back.' The girl who appeared to be the leader spoke at last. Her tone was contemptuous and the effect immediate. Pex's performance collapsed completely and he stood shamefacedly by Mel's side. The Blue Kangs had not even bothered to respond physically to Pex's challenge.

'Will you please tell us why you're holding us here?' Mel demanded.

'We saw you with the Red Kangs,' the Blue Kang leader replied.

61

'Yes,' Mel acknowledged, 'but they were holding me captive too. 'I don't know much about them. I'm certainly not their friend.' The Blue Kangs appeared undecided so Mel persisted. 'Look, my name's Mel. I'm just a visitor here.'

The Blue Kang nodded curtly at Pex. 'You know him?'

'I'm protecting her,' Pex put in aggressively before Mel could reply. His intervention irritated Mel and it gave her an ideal opportunity to find out more about someone who had dogged her steps ever since she'd been parted from the Doctor. 'Do you know this person?' she asked.

'All Kangs know the Musclebrain,' the Blue Kang leader answered, with a mocking smile. 'Scaredy cat Pex. When the in-betweens sent us all here in the Ship, us and the oldsters, the Musclebrain hid away and came with us. 'Cos he didn't want to fight in the war along with the other in-betweens.'

'Who told you that?' Pex spoke sharply but he had a shifty look in his eye and Mel already started to suspect the Blue Kang was telling the truth.

'Everyone knows that,' she replied, choosing to address herself to Mel and ignoring Pex. 'The oldsters call out after him in the carrydoors. The Musclebrain is a scaredy cat.'

'Scaredy cat! Scaredy cat!' The other Kangs took up the cry and clustered round the unhappy Pex. His eyes took on a haunted look.

'Is this true, Pex?' At first there was no reply. Mel asked again and finally Pex acknowledged that it was true. Every word of it.

'I've made up for it since I was here,' he insisted, desperately. 'Since I've been in Paradise Towers, I've been brave, a hero, a fighting mach –' he stopped, unable to continue.

Mel could not keep the sarcasm out of her voice. 'Sent by powers you weren't allowed to name?' she reminded him. Then added bitterly, 'I should have guessed.' If she had ever been uncertain whether she was better off on her own, there could be no doubt now.

She turned to the Blue Kang leader. 'Will you allow me to

go if I go alone? I give you my word I mean no harm. You can see I've got no weapons, nothing dangerous. Look.'

She held out her arms to show her defencelessness. There was a tense moment while the leader glanced round the others for approval of Mel's proposal but there was no hostility or distrust in their young faces.

'You may go.'

'Thanks.'

There was only the painful moment of saying goodbye to Pex before Mel could go. She was tempted just to walk away but he was so dejected that she felt she had to say something. 'Goodbye, Pex,' she said sadly. 'I'm sorry for you.'

And then Mel was off alone down the street. The taunting cries of 'Scaredy cat' gradually faded from her ears.

Maddy was one of the younger Rezzies. Plumper, jollier and, in many ways, more innocent than her two elderly near neighbours. But she noticed things and she listened to things. And there were a lot of rumours going the rounds of the Rezzies which were disturbing enough to keep her awake at night. In the end, she had decided that she ought to go and talk it all over with Tilda and Tabby. They were, after all, older and wiser than she was, and might put it all in perspective. The only problem was that they didn't always encourage calls, indeed were sometimes distinctly unwelcoming. So it was with some trepidation that she knocked on their front door. Or what was left of it.

'Come in!' Tilda's voice called welcomingly. Maddy stepped in eagerly but was almost immediately aware of an air of disappointment. She strongly suspected they had been expecting someone else.

'I hope I'm not intruding,' Maddy began.

'No, no,' Tabby replied. 'We're just finishing.' She picked the last piece of meat off a small carcase that lay on the table. Its shape and size fascinated Maddy. Meat, after all, was a rare treat now that times were so hard in Paradise Towers. It might even be a rat. Or a very large mouse. She envied them

63

whatever it was. She rarely had the nerve to set traps herself.

Tilda saw her staring at the carcase and in a trice the plate had been whisked away. 'Have some tea, Maddy,' Tilda put in, to cover the activity.

'Oh, thank you, dear,' Maddy replied, settling herself into a seat at the table by Tabby. Tabby always made her nervous. She couldn't tell why. Maybe it was those protruding teeth. Nevertheless, Tabby smiled amiably enough while Tilda bustled around making tea.

'I just had to come and tell you.'

'Tell us what, Maddy?'

'Another Caretaker's disappeared.' She delivered the latest rumour with some pride. It wasn't often that she knew something Tilda and Tabby didn't. But the item fell rather flat. The older Rezzies only evinced a modicum of interest.

'Was it the Kangs?' Tabby enquired, picking something from her large front teeth.

'Well,' Maddy replied, 'they're trying to make out it might be.' She leant forward conspiratorially. 'But from what I've heard, there's more to it than anybody's letting on. I mean, people don't just vanish, do they?'

'Oh no, of course not. There's always something left behind.' Rather an odd remark of Tilda's, Maddy thought. Odder still since as she spoke she was pouring the bones left over from the meal into the waste disposal unit in the wall. It made a rather alarming gurgling noise as the bones disappeared into its metal jaws.

'You know, Tilda and Tabby, my dears,' Maddy continued over the din, trying once again to turn the conversation the way she wanted. 'I do sometimes wonder if we know everything that's going on in dear Paradise Towers.'

'What do you mean?' Tabby was puzzled rather than interested.

There was so much that Maddy wanted to discuss. The missing Caretakers. The strange noises she sometimes heard coming from Tilda and Tabby's flat. The severe shortage of meat all the Rezzies were experiencing and some tips on how to remedy the deficiency. But, somehow, when it came to it, she didn't have the nerve.

'Oh, I don't know,' she tailed off vaguely; 'It's just a feeling. I'm probably being silly.'

Tilda and Tabby made no comment. But that was hardly surprising. Their minds were quite elsewhere. Wondering whether that delicious little Mel would ever come back to see them again.

It was the high point of the Chief Caretaker's day. He was going to visit his pet. After the Deputy Chief's bungling, he deserved a treat. He had taken the special Mark UT Service Lift down to the Basement and he was walking along the long familiar dark basement corridor to where his pet was kept. Others might have found the slimy corridors unwelcoming or even alarming. The Chief Caretaker, however, was used to them and hummed to himself as he went.

His humming stopped all of a sudden. Lying on the grimy floor in front of him was something he did not understand. It was an item of clothing. It had once belonged to a Red Kang. And it was blood-stained. The Chief picked it up to examine it more closely. Caretaker number 345 stroke 12 subsection 3 he remembered. The last of the Yellow Kangs he remembered. But a Red Kang? He had had nothing to do with that.

He took the scrap of cloth and marched purposefully on. He would have to have words with his pet. Explanations were in order.

As he approached the end of the corridor, heavy studded doors flew open. From the room inside billowed clouds of smoke. The Chief was used to what lay beyond the door but it still roused in him feelings of awe. Through the smoke he could see the two fiery red unblinking eyes that were all that was visible of his pet, his pride and joy, the chief resident of the Basement.

'Hello, my pet, how are you?' The Chief's voice was jaunty but the red eyes were unnervingly bright and piercing today. 'Did you enjoy your nice Caretaker?'

He listened carefully. His pet usually communicated through a dull mechanical throb. It always reminded the Chief of the waste disposal units fitted in all the flats in the Towers. When he had first made the acquaintance of his little treasure, the Chief had heard nothing in its throbbing but simple mechanical sounds. Now he could often make out words. Or, at least, what sounded like words. It might be his imgaination, of course. It might simply be that he had got more used to interpreting the noises his pet made. Or, as the Chief believed was most likely, his pet was starting to grow and develop. And with that development came a voice. It spoke now.

'Hungry . . .'

'Hungry!' the Chief was almost indignant. 'You can't be. Daddy's always made sure you've had a good supply of what you need. Daddy's the Chief Caretaker – that's his main job.'

'Hungry.' The throbbing voice was growing in power. The Chief had to take the initiative now before things got out of hand. He held up the scrap of Red Kang clothing.

'While we're on the subject, Daddy's not too pleased with you. Now I didn't send you this little snack, did I?' He waved the blood-stained cloth in front of the flashing eyes. 'I mean, the Cleaners don't do things like that without orders from someone. And it wasn't me.' The Chief's voice took on a pleading tone. 'So who was it? Now tell Daddy.'

There was no reply. Even the demand to be fed was momentarily stilled. There was just a low throbbing. The lack of response was too much for the Chief and he finally snapped. 'If you don't tell Daddy who's been feeding you behind his back, I won't give you the Great Architect to eat.'

'Hungry!!!' There was a sudden angry roar and the throbbing voice returned even more powerfully than before. Its power was indeed rather terrifying.

The Chief began to feel for the very first time that he was out of his depth. This was no ordinary pet any more. It had a will and hunger of its own.

'Hungry!!!'

'All right, all right.' The Chief was conciliatory now. He

66

could feel his eyelid starting to twitch with tension and he was trying very hard to control it. 'You'll get the Great Architect just as soon as I can catch him again.'

'Hungry!!! Hungry!!!'

The voice was bellowing now and the Chief was practically deafened. His pet was not normally like this. If only his darling would confide in Daddy all would be well. Or would it? The Chief was no longer sure. This hunger seemed beyond his control. Perhaps beyond anyone's control.

The feeling that all was not as it should be in Paradise Towers hit the Chief again with a still more devastating force.

6

Brainquarters

The Doctor's eyes opened. He had no idea where he was or how he had got there. For the moment his surroundings were a blur. He waited for them to get clearer.

'Build High for Happiness, Doctor!'

The voice was familiar. And the face too now that the Doctor had managed to focus on it. It belonged to Bin Liner. She was peering down at him with an amused expression on her face. And next to her the Doctor made out the face of Fire Escape. Crossbows at the ready, he noted, even in his fuddled state.

The Doctor sat up, still rubbing his head, and started to look about him. It was gloomy but the Doctor could make out several rows of bunk beds, piles of food and supplies, a stack of crossbows. And a whole line of Red Kangs standing just a little way off, eyeing him warily.

'What's happened?'

'You dropped down, Doctor,' Fire Escape replied. 'Whoosh into our Brainquarters.' She paused. 'Where is the girl who is not a Kang?'

'I only wish I knew,' sighed the Doctor. He got to his feet, brushed himself down and replaced his hat firmly on his head. No bones broken, he noted thankfully. He was starting to feel better already. 'Fire Escape, Bin Liner,' he continued cheerfully, 'I never expected to see you again. Still less did I expect to be glad to see you again. But I've got to go. There's much to be done.'

He knew he was being optimistic believing the Red Kangs would let him go just like that. It was worth the try nevertheless. But his optimism was not to be rewarded. Kang crossbows were raised and pointed.

'No way.'

'No ball games. No flyposts. No outgoing.'

Bin Liner studied the Doctor carefully. 'Why you here?'

'It's an accident,' the Doctor replied. 'I was being chased by two Cleaners and – '

'Cleaners?' Fire Escape tensed visibly.

'Yes,' the Doctor answered. 'I expect they'll have gone by now.'

'Check for safe and sure on the talkiphone.' Bin Liner nodded and went over to the talkiphone. To the Doctor's surprise this one too was like a large drinks dispenser such as were common on Mel's Earth. But he had more immediate problems than finding out how it worked. While Bin Liner was punching out a code and listening for the report of Kang Eye-Spy, he had a cluster of Kang crossbows still aimed at his person.

'Do I get the impression I'm not believed, Fire Escape?'

'Cleaners make Kangs unalive.'

'Oh, do they now?' The Doctor's eyes gleamed. 'Why don't you tell me about it?' But Fire Escape dropped her eyes, avoiding his gaze. Once again, he was up against the wall of silence that seemed to hem him in at every turn in Paradise Towers. The Doctor had had enough.

'What is the matter with everyone in the Towers?' he demanded. 'I simply don't understand it. I mean, the Cleaners go round killing people and carting them off and no-one does anything to stop them. All you Kangs do is draw wallscrawls on the subject all over the place. And the Caretakers are no better. They allow themselves to be killed off without saying anything just because there's nothing about it in their precious rule book. I happen to know that because I've read it.'

His words finally had an effect. Fire Escape's jaw dropped and she stared at the Doctor wide-eyed. 'You mean, there's a wipe-out of Caretakers as well?'

'Don't tell me you don't know,' the Doctor mocked, pushing

his advantage. 'I mean, what is going on?' He reached for his pocket book and flourished his sketches under Fire Escape's nose. 'What, for example, is behind that door belching out smoke that you Kangs are so keen on painting pictures of, eh? Any ideas? Or is that simply just another mystery?'

Fire Escape was spared the embarrassment of replying because at this moment Bin Liner had put down the talkiphone and was ready to report. But the Doctor knew he had rattled the Kangs. There was at least a chance that, carefully handled, they might start to trust him enough to take him into their confidence.

'Cleaners were in the carrydoor. With sprinkle gas. There no more.'

The Eye-Spy's report made everyone relax. The crossbows were lowered and the Doctor no longer under immediate threat. But rather than pressing on too quickly with his investigations and losing the Kang's confidence again, the Doctor took a more devious path. He asked if he could take a look at the talkiphone. Bin Liner nodded agreement but watched warily as the Doctor approached the machine.

The Doctor smiled secretly. His impression had been correct. There was even a label reading 'Fizzade' on the front. 'You know, you really are very stupid for such clever people,' he continued as he took in the Kang's ingenious telephone technology. 'If I were you, I'd find that door that belches smoke and discover what's behind it. Because, until you do, we're all at risk – you, me, Mel, everybody.' The Kangs said nothing but he knew they were taking in what he was saying.

'This is really a splendid piece of auditory-architechnotonical metrosyncosthopy,' the Doctor added casually, almost as an afterthought, holding up the talkiphone receiver.

'It works,' Fire Escape replied warily.

'However, you probably haven't realised that this machine has another purpose.' The Kangs eyed him suspiciously. The Doctor reached in his pocket and pulled out one of the coins he had discovered by the Emergency phone upstairs.

'Incidentally,' he remarked, 'yet another Paradise Towers mystery. The coin reads "issued by the Great Architect Kroagnon". I only wish I could place the name. And what has happened to him since he finished this building? No one seems to know.'

But he sensed the Kangs were waiting for his experiment with the talkiphone. Speculation would have to wait. He inserted the coin in the rusted slot in the drinks machine, selected 'Orange Fizzade' on the selector panel and pressed the 'Deliver' button. He just hoped the machine was still in working order or else his little performance to impress the Kangs would fall rather flat.

The machine started to judder and rattle. The mystified Kangs instinctively backed away in alarm. The Doctor, however, held his ground. And, to his considerable relief, a bright orange can of Fizzade clattered out of the machine and into his waiting hands. He pulled off the metal tab and took a long swig. It was actually very good orangeade and, after his recent mishaps, very refreshing. He took another swig.

The Kangs still held back but were undoubtedly impressed. He offered the can to Bin Liner. She hesitated at first, but, having seen the Docor drink first, decided to take the risk. She took a small sip and the others gathered round to see the result. She liked what she tasted and quickly gulped some more.

'Icehot, Doctor,' she announced approvingly.

Then all the Kangs wanted to drink and the Doctor was kept busy feeding the machine with coins to keep them supplied with further Fizzade. There was an air of relaxation, almost celebration, in the Brainquarters. The Doctor's ploy had paid off. They would trust him more now he felt. And respect his skills.

'Icehot!' The cry went round the group as they drank. The Doctor had achieved something potentially very valuable, but, for the moment, the big unanswered questions about the Towers would have to wait.

'So you still haven't discovered where the Great Architect has got to?'

71

'No, Chief.'

'And you have no idea of his whereabouts at all?'

'No, Chief, unless –'

'Unless?' The Chief was back at his Headquarters now and taking out his growing anxiety about his pet on the cowering and sweating Deputy Chief.

'Unless he was taken by the Cleaners.' The Deputy brought out the words reluctantly, barely able to bring his eyes to meet those of his superior.

'Don't be absurd.' The Chief was sharp and dismissive. He had to be if the Deputy didn't start getting hold of ideas that could create considerable problems for the Chief's relation with his subordinates. 'You are overlooking one very obvious possibility.'

'What's that, Chief?'

'The Wallscrawlers, of course,' the Chief snapped. 'They've been getting very bold of late and making fun of authority.' He made a sudden decision. 'Summon all available Caretakers. We are going to start a 45D Section 3 Security Search.'

'Yes, Chief.'

The Chief Caretaker's bloodshot eyes glinted. 'The 327 Appendix 3 Subsection 9 Death of the Great Architect must take place. And, besides,' he added, 'even if the Wallscrawlers don't have him, it's high time they were taught a severe lesson.'

A few minutes later the 45D Section 3 Security Search was under way. The Deputy had brought out the G9H Suspect Tracker, the pride of the Caretakers' armoury of gadgets. An image of the suspect, the Doctor in this case, was given to the Tracker and the Tracker did the rest, tracing the wanted person through Paradise Towers until it had brought him to ground, wherever he might be hiding. The G9H Suspect Tracker, a considerable improvement on the G8H, had a very high success rate. And the Deputy needed success. He had no doubt who would pay the price if the Doctor was not found. He must not fail the Chief again.

In short, the Deputy Chief, backed by the G9H Suspect

Tracker, drills, gadgets, weapons, and the toughest and strongest of the Caretakers, was on the Doctor's trail.

'Cooee! Care for a cup of tea?'

Mel gave a start. Since she had left Pex, she had been almost in a daze, taking turnings and choosing staircases without any real sense of where she was going. She had just hoped that persistence might change her luck. But surely that couldn't be Tilda's voice. She couldn't be back at the Rezzies' flat yet again?

But she *was* back at the flat and there could be no doubt that it was indeed Tilda standing there in her doorway, as before, smiling welcomingly.

'It's lovely to see you again,' Tilda beamed. 'We'd almost given up hope. How have you been getting on?'

'Not very well,' Mel sighed. 'I seem to have been going round and round in circles.'

Tilda was all commiseration. 'Oh, what a shame! Why don't you come inside and rest your weary bones?'

Mel hesitated. She was torn. She felt strongly that she should carry on and find the Doctor. And somewhere inside her an alarm bell was going off, warning her that it was not a good idea to accept Tilda's invitation. But, on the other hand, she *was* very tired. If she didn't rest for a while, have something to eat and drink, she would collapse from exhaustion in some dingy corner of the Towers, which would be no help either to the Doctor or herself.

So she accepted. 'Just for a moment, mind,' she insisted, 'to get my strength back.'

Tilda, needless to say, was delighted. She hustled Mel eagerly into her flat before Mel had a chance to re-consider. As they entered, Tabby looked up from a long piece of knitting she was working on.

'Tabby,' trilled Tilda, excitedly. 'Guess what, a real piece of good fortune. You'll never guess who's arrived for tea. Mel!'

And Tabby smiled welcomingly too. Mel had forgotten about the long, sharp front teeth until now. If she'd remembered them, she might not have been so easily persuaded to come in for tea. But then she was probably being silly. And, besides, Tilda was bustling about eagerly preparing the tea things, humming happily to herself. And Tabby was beckoning to Mel to sit beside her. It was too late now.

'Build High for Happiness, Doctor!'

'And Build High for Happiness to you too.'

The party atmosphere was still prevailing in Red Kang Brainquarters. 'We always knew we liked you, Doctor,' Fire Escape confided, 'because of your high fabshion clothes.'

'Thank you,' the Doctor returned, amiably. 'But let us not lose sight of what we have to do. We must find Mel, my friend, and solve the mystery of Paradise Towers because I have learnt enough to know that its very existence is at stake.'

'Icehot, Doctor, icehot,' Bin Liner agreed. The Kangs were always pleased when there was a scent of adventure in the air. And now they had heard what the Doctor had to say and seen his prodigious conjuring act with the talkiphone, they were beginning to understand that they had to take action or else. If even Caretakers were being made unalive, something very odd indeed was going on.

The Kangs raised their cans to celebrate their new-found understanding once more and the Doctor returned the toast for the umpteenth time, wondering once again where the phrase 'Build High for Happiness' came from. Another little mystery to add to the others.

Then a warning alarm went off. Its strident ringing shattered the hilarity in an instant. The Kangs were alert again, discarded crossbows back in their hands. Bin Liner ran to a periscope-like peephole to see what was going on at floor level above.

When she removed her eye from the peephole, her face was stern. 'I can see Caretakers.' She turned grimly to the Doctor.

'Ware Doctor!'

The mood was ugly now. The Doctor was no longer the Kangs' friend. 'He brings them here,' said Fire Escape, pointing accusingly. 'Because, like Caretakers, he wants all Wallscrawlers unalive.'

'Not at all. You don't understand,' protested the Doctor. 'I mean, the last people I want to meet are the Caretakers. I'd be in as much danger as you are. More, probably.' He looked round the circle of suspicious young faces. 'You've got to believe me. We've got to work together. The Chief Caretaker is off his head. If we don't stop the wipeouts, who will?'

The alarm kept ringing. The Doctor had to raise his voice to be heard above it. 'Please,' he pleaded. Then the alarm ended its piercing warning and there was quiet for a moment. And in the quiet, another sound became audible. The distant sound of a powerful drill. The Caretakers must be drilling into the door. They would soon be down in the Brainquarters.

The Kangs stood momentarily paralysed, unable to decide what to do. 'You must have a secret escape route,' the Doctor urged. 'It's not like Kangs to allow themselves to be caught like rats in a trap.'

'Red Kangs have an unseen outway,' Bin Liner acknowledged. 'But –'

'But what?'

'The Caretakers will be in our Brainquarters too soon for the Kangs to use it.' She glanced regretfully towards the concealed outway which a couple of the Kangs had started to uncover.

'I see,' the Doctor said, 'you need time?'

Bin Liner nodded. And at that moment, the Doctor made his decision. 'I will buy you the time,' he announced. 'I'm the reason why the Caretakers are here. Go on. Make your escape while you can.'

The Kangs still stared. 'It's not like Kangs to be so slow, is it? Go *on*.'

And then almost as if they were parts of one being, the Kangs started to move. Within seconds they were gathered at the concealed outway in an orderly file. And in not much more time they were through the hole and out of sight. Bin Liner, the last, pulled the covering back over the hole.

The Doctor was alone in the Kang Brainquarters. The

drilling sounds were getting louder. The Caretakers would be there in a few minutes. The Doctor had made his choice and he had to live with it. He sat down to wait.

7

Come into My Parlour

'You feeling better now, dear?'

'Yes, thank you. There's nothing quite like tea and crumpets is there? I feel so much more relaxed.'

It was true. Mel was feeling nicely drowsy but a lot better for Tilda and Tabby's hospitality. Tabby had toasted crumpets on a large metal toasting fork over a fire. And Tilda had provided seemingly endless amounts of cream and cakes for her to eat.

'Oh, it's so good to hear you're relaxed, dear. Isn't it, Tilda?'

'Very good,' Tilda agreed.

'All the same,' Mel began, 'I really must be going now.' She was so comfortable in her armchair that it did seem a pity to drag herself away but she knew she had to if she was ever to meet up with the Doctor.

She started to rise from her chair but Tabby gently restrained her.

'We couldn't possibly let you go,' she said, her hand tightening on Mel's arm in a slightly alarming way.

'Oh, no, not this time,' Tilda put in. 'We can't possibly miss this opportunity, can we, Tabby?'

'No, we can't, Tilda. Not since those horrid little Kangs got suspicious of our little ways.'

'I am sorry dear.' There was a regretful look in Tilda's eye and Tabby's grip had not lessened in force one jot. Mel watched mesmerised. She didn't understand what they were talking about. Or, rather, perhaps she did and couldn't quite believe it. The bones. The fattening up. Tabby's rat teeth. Surely not.

'What do you mean?' she demanded, trying to control a

slight tremor in her voice.

'Well, you see, dear,' Tilda answered sweetly, 'we would like you to stay. For a very long time.'

'In fact,' cooed Tabby, 'we don't imagine you ever leaving at all.'

'You are joking, aren't you?' Mel strove to control the rising panic. If this was a nightmare she couldn't wait to wake up. But no, Tilda and Tabby were there and regarding her hungrily. Hungrily. There was no other word for it.

'I'm afraid we're not joking,' Tilda insisted gravely. 'We don't see this as a matter for humour. We mean every word.'

Mel tried to rise but Tabby's hand pinned her to the chair. Tilda meanwhile had grabbed hold of some of Tabby's knitting and now she threw it over Mel. Mel struggled but it was hopeless. The old ladies were surprisingly strong and wiry and in a few moments she was trussed up like a turkey.

'In our experience, Mel dear,' Tilda was saying as the Rezzies completed their task, 'it is much better not to struggle. It only causes needless distress.'

And then the old ladies were bustling all over the kitchen, bringing out utensils of all sorts, chopping boards, saucepans, spices. It even looked as if Tabby's toasting fork had more than one use. And the waste disposal unit was starting to throb loudly again just to add to the ghoulishness of the spectacle.

'Look,' Mel pleaded, 'a joke's a joke but this has gone on long enough.'

Tilda paused for a moment in her preparations. 'Mel, dear, I do think by now you should appreciate the fact that, though Tabby and myself are not averse to a humorous remark now and then, no joke is intended.' And, having finally damped down Mel's last flickering hopes, she returned to her work. 'Can you spot the basil anywhere, Tabby?'

Tabby fumbled in the cupboard. 'It's here somewhere.'

Mel sat in despair. And then something very peculiar happened. A large white claw emerged from the waste disposal chute. It snapped open and shut silently a few times, as if searching for something, and then popped back out of sight letting the flap on the disposal system fall back into place.

Mel stared. And continued to stare. She couldn't really believe she had seen what she was seeing. An involuntary cry came from her lips.

'What is it dear?' Tabby was all attention.

'I think there's something wrong with the waste disposal unit.'

'Don't talk nonsense, dear. It always makes that funny noise.'

'But I think I saw something come up it,' Mel insisted.

'Don't be silly.'

'We'd better make sure, Tabby,' put in Tilda, busy chopping up vegetables.

'Oh, very well, dear.' Tabby gave a weary sigh and approached the chute. Mel watched her but Tilda carried on with her preparations, her back turned away from the proceedings, concentrating hard on her task.

Tabby peered at the unit. It was very noisy. Far noisier than usual. And the control panel light was flashing in an erratic way. But nothing unusual was visible.

'I can't see anything, Tilda,' she announced. And then, just to make sure, she opened the flap to take a closer look. Mel tried to shout out but it was too late. The metal claw had already shot out and fastened itself round Tabby's throat. She didn't even have time to cry out.

Mel watched, horrified. In a few seconds the claw had whisked the bulky Rezzie up off her feet and dragged her down the chute. She disappeared with one final cry. And then the flap closed. Tabby was hurtling down the chute to whatever lay in wait at the bottom of the Towers.

Tilda heard the noise and turned. In a flash she realised Tabby was no longer there. She rushed to the chute and lifted the flap to look down.

'Tabby! Tabby!' Tilda's voice became a wail as she realised her companion was gone for good. But she did not waste time on grief. Instead, she turned on Mel, her face a mask of fury. The kitchen knife she was still holding glinted ominously in her hand. Mel instinctively cowered back.

'Oh, what a naughty little girl we are!' Tabby hissed furiously. 'Looks as though butter wouldn't melt in her mouth and now she's killed poor dear Tabby.'

'It wasn't me, Tilda,' Mel protested. 'It was the thing in the waste disposal unit that –' her voice trailed away. Tilda was so bent on getting revenge for her loss that she was quite beyond listening to reason or logic.

'Fibbing too, is it now?' she spat. 'I hate little fibbers.' She started to advance menacingly, kitchen knife in hand. Mel continued to shrink back but she was tied so tight there was little she could do to avoid Tilda's murderous advance. Mel prepared herself for the end.

And then behind her back there was a loud splintering noise oddly familiar to Mel's ears. With a gasp she realised what it meant. Pex had broken down the door again and was standing posed in the doorway.

'My name is Pex and –'

But he failed to finish. Firstly, there were Mel's desperate screams for help to contend with. And then there was the sight of Tilda balefully staring at him, her intentions all too clearly written on her face. And the knife in her hand in the process of being raised to impale him against the door.

'Oh no, now look –' Pex gulped ineffectually as he realised what he had walked into. This was real danger. Not at all what he had had in mind. But again his sentence was cut short. Tilda viciously threw her knife at him. Pex only managed to duck just in time. And the knife whistled past his ear and stuck quivering in what was left of the door.

'Help!' Mel screamed again but Pex was too petrified to move. And now Tilda was moving back to the chute to pick up Tabby's huge toasting fork to throw that at him. She grabbed it and started to take aim.

Pex gulped in horror and pointed behind her. To Tilda this was just a feeble ploy to break her concentration and she ignored him. But it was not a ploy at all. The claw that had so terrified Mel had reappeared from behind the flap and was snapping greedily at Tilda's back.

The Rezzie drew back her arm to take aim at Pex. The sweat was running from his brow now. And then just as her arm was pulled back to its fullest extent, the claw pounced. Tilda overbalanced with a cry and was dragged in seconds into the unit and down the chute. The lights on the machine flashed ominously for a few moments. And then the unit juddered to a halt and all was quiet.

There was a pause. Neither Mel nor Pex moved. Until finally Pex came to his senses and started to help Mel disentangle herself from the Rezzies' knitting.

'You arrived just in time,' Mel gasped as she struggled free at last, scarcely able to believe her luck.

'Mel –'

'Yes, Pex –'

Pex's jaw was set and his features frozen in thought. When he spoke it was for once very tentatively. 'Mel, does this mean that I've really helped save somebody from something? For the very first time.'

Mel grinned at him affectionately. 'I think it might.'

It was the first time she had seen Pex smile.

The drilling was complete and the exhausted Caretaker ready to push in the door. The Deputy Chief stepped forward officiously.

'I think you'll find the Rule Book states that I remove the last section of the door,' he announced. The other Caretakers dutifully stepped back. The Deputy gave a vicious kick and the remnants of the door fell into the darkness below. The Deputy stuck his head into the aperture and looked down.

'Greetings, Deputy Chief Caretaker!' There at the bottom of a steep flight of dark stairs the Deputy made out the figure of the Doctor. He couldn't really believe the evidence of his own eyes.

'You look surprised to see me,' the Doctor continued cheerily from the depths of the Kang Brainquarters. 'I can't imagine why. I thought it was me you were looking for.'

81

'Seize him!' A couple of the burliest Caretakers stumbled down the steps and brought the Doctor back up. It was hard work, given the steepness of the steps, but the Doctor made no resistance. His very compliance made the slow-witted Deputy suspicious.

'You're not alone down there, are you?' the Deputy asked when the Doctor had been placed face to face with him at street level.

'Well, as a matter of fact, I am,' the Doctor returned amiably. 'I found this cosy little hole just by accident, some sort of broom cupboard I suppose, but ideal for a quick snooze.'

'You don't fool me, Great Architect,' the Deputy snapped back. 'There are Kangs down there.'

'Take a look for yourself if you don't believe me.'

The Doctor gestured courteously to the gaping hole that led down to the Brainquarters. The Deputy, whose dim brain always suspected people were trying to make a fool of him, accepted the challenge. He went down into the Brainquarters. He searched under bunk beds and inside cupboards. He upturned boxes filled with food. And he stuck his head into the Fizzade machine. But he found nothing.

It was a weary Deputy who came back up the stairs to see the Doctor grinning pleasantly. 'Well, Deputy Chief?'

The Deputy Chief made no attempt to conceal how peeved he was. 'I don't know what you're so pleased about,' he said with a grim smile, 'There's a 327 Appendix 3 Subsection 9 Death waiting for you.' He turned to the waiting retinue of Caretakers. 'Bring him back to Headquarters.'

And, not for the first time, the Doctor found himself being bundled off down shadowy streets for an encounter with the Chief Caretaker. He was not to know that this time his journey was being monitored by bright young Red Kang eyes. Kangs never forgot a favour.

The Rezzies seemed to have never thrown anything away. In the cupboards and drawers of their flat, neatly stacked away, were bizarre-looking mouse traps, balls of string, quantities of cooking utensils, any number of varieties of birdseed. And specially wrapped in a lovingly knitted woollen holder was what Mel had been looking for.

'What is it?' Pex asked as Mel held it up triumphantly. He was still recovering from his ordeal and lacked Mel's energy for investigation.

'It's a map of Paradise Towers,' Mel replied. 'It occurred to me that when everybody was first sent here they would have been given a map to help them get around.'

'I wasn't,' Pex protested but then he stopped and blushed. 'But then – well, nobody knew I was in the ship, did they?'

Mel, however, was too busy unfolding the map on to the biggest of the glass-topped tables to notice his embarrassment. As she carefully spread out the map, smoothing out the folds, the whole shape of Paradise Towers was clear before her for the first time. She was thankful the Rezzies had been such hoarders.

Pex came over to see.

'Now at last we can see where we are,' Mel said, as her eyes took in the scale of the whole architectural undertaking. 'It's huge isn't it? Three hundred and four floors.' She pointed to a neat mark Tilda or Tabby had made indicating their flat. 'That shows we must be on floor one hundred and nine.'

'Mel –'

'Yes?'

'Are you sure you want to get to the pool in the sky?'

'Of course,' Mel returned. 'That's where I'm meeting the Doctor.'

'You musn't go.' Pex's face had taken on the hunted look Mel remembered from when he had been cornered by the Blue Kangs.

'Don't be silly, Pex.' She consulted the map. 'Look, there it is, on the map. Floor three hundred and four. What's the point of having a pool if no-one ever uses it?'

'But, Mel –' Pex persisted, 'only the unalive go there.'

'Who says so?'

'Everybody.' Pex blushed again. 'Bin Liner and Fire Escape.'

'Well, after being attacked by Kangs and nearly eaten by Tilda and Tabby, I can't see that I can possibly be in more danger up there than down here,' Mel scoffed. 'Might even have a swim if I'm lucky.' She broke off as her sharp eyes spotted something else on the map. 'Now that's odd.'

'What?'

'Look down there.' Mel pointed to the bottom-most section of the map. 'Basement' the legend read. And then right across the section, practically obliterating all details of its layout had been printed the words, 'Entry Forbidden to All Residents of Paradise Towers on Pain of Death.'

Pex gulped. 'Well,' Mel said, determined to look on the bright side, 'at least it sounds as if it's safer going up than going down. You needn't come if you don't want to, Pex.'

'But I do.' Pex's face was anxious but still resolute. 'It's my job to protect you.'

Knowing how fearful Pex was, Mel tried to persuade him to think again. After all, he had saved her life once now, didn't that mean he had done enough? But Pex could be very obstinate when he wanted to be as Mel had already learned. And after recent events, she was secretly quite glad that he might tag along. She was beginning to feel quite fond of this muddled-headed, cowardly, self-appointed vigilante.

'So you're coming with me, come what may?' Mel asked finally.

Pex nodded. The discussion was over. Mel started to fold up the map to take with them. It would transform their journey. She didn't imagine it was going to be easy. But for the first time she really believed they could make it to the great pool in the sky.

'Welcome back, Great Architect.' The Chief turned from the bank of screens in his Headquarters to face the Doctor who was bundled into his presence by the proud Deputy.

The Chief's bloodshot eyes took in the prisoner gloatingly. 'I'm relieved that it's you and not my Deputy who will be enjoying the 327 Appendix 3 Subsection 9 death. For a start,

84

his demise would have involved an enormous amount of extra paperwork.'

'Chief–' The Deputy had picked up bad news from his Mark 12 LDCE on the journey home and wanted to discuss it. 'Chief, just now I heard reports that Caretaker number 97 stroke 2 subsection 9 has disappeared without any known explanation and that Caretaker number 348 stroke –'

'I'm well aware of that,' the Chief cut in brusquely.

'But, Chief,' the Deputy continued, too concerned to notice the Chief's growing impatience. 'If this goes on and the Cleaners *are* out of control, how many of us are going to be left?'

There was a deathly silence. The Deputy stopped, shame-faced. He had gone too far and he knew it even before the Chief started to reply in a hushed but stern voice.

'Deputy Chief Caretaker, by talking out of turn in such a way, you have just broken so many rules and regulations that it would take several hours just to enumerate them.' The Deputy bowed his head.

'Wait outside.'

'Yes, Chief.'

'And that goes for the rest of you,' the Chief added, daring the other Caretakers to pick up the baton of protest his Deputy had so quickly dropped. There were no takers, he noted with relief. The Chief's searching gaze turned back to the Doctor. 'I think it would be a good idea if before his death, the Great Architect and I had a nice little Regulation 13 Appendix 2 Final Conversation.'

Moments later the Doctor and the Chief were alone in the control room. Two strong wills confronted each other in silence. The Doctor decided he would wait for the Chief to start. If he was to die anyway, he might as well see what the Chief had in mind in sending his subordinates all away so peremptorily. The Doctor was fairly certain there were things the Chief had to say which were not for the ears of the already rattled Caretakers.

'Are you the Great Architect?' The Chief suddenly broke his broody silence.

'You mean, you're not certain any more?'

'Oh, I shall kill you anyway,' the Chief put in, 'but it would be interesting to know.'

'What makes you think I am the Great Architect anyway?' the Doctor enquired. 'Haven't you ever met him?'

The Chief shook his head. 'Just when Paradise Towers was being completed, before any of us got here, he disappeared under mysterious circumstances. He's never been seen since. Anywhere.

'How odd.' The Doctor was deliberately non-committal, waiting for more.

'Odd indeed,' agreed the Chief, 'for a being whose head was apparently full of extravagant future plans.' He stared balefully at the Doctor. 'But I always knew in my bones that he'd turn up again one day. And start altering things just when I'd got them the way I wanted.'

'And that would justify killing me – I mean him?'

'Oh yes.' There was not a scrap of remorse or doubt in the Chief's voice. The Doctor felt now was the time for him to take the initiative. Not least because he could feel anger building up inside him against the Chief's cynical ruthlessness.

He fixed his adversary with a steely look. 'Like everyone else in Paradise Towers,' he began, 'you seem terrified to face up to the reality of what's happening here. I mean, killing me won't help you to find out who is sending those robotic cleaners out to kill people. You've certainly got your Deputy and all the other Caretakers thoroughly scared for their lives. And that's a problem which isn't going to go away.' The Chief was returning his gaze steadily up to now but the Doctor suddenly took a leap into the unexpected. 'Unless, of course, you're giving all those orders yourself.'

'A ridiculous idea!' The Chief's dismissive reaction was immediate but there was something shifty and nervous about the way his eyes were starting to move. The Doctor gained the confidence to carry on.

'Ridiculous perhaps. But I do have a better one.'

'And what is that?'

The Doctor took his time now, choosing his words carefully. 'Of course,' he began brightly, 'there can be no doubt you have been allowing the Cleaners to kill off *some* of your people, as well, of course, as any poor innocent Kangs they can find, for reasons that are, for the moment, beyond me. But then I'm not a power-crazed psychopath.'

'What did you say?' The Chief was furious and his voice echoed round the room. But the Doctor kept his head. The more the Chief blustered, the more certain he became he was on the right track.

'Look, Chief Caretaker, you're going to kill me anyway so you may as well make use of my brain, for what it's worth, while I'm here.' The Chief saw the force of this and subsided back into his chair as the Doctor continued: 'What I also think is happening here, besides your own activities, is that Caretakers, Kangs, Red, Blue, Yellow, anyone in sight is being killed off *without* any instructions from you. And without any reference whatsoever to that precious rule book of yours.' He paused. 'And that's why you're worried. You don't know who's doing it.'

'Oh, don't I?' The Chief had been listening intently up to now but the last thrust was too much. His sallow face went red with rage and he rose angrily from his seat. The Doctor had touched a nerve all right.

At that moment the Chief was furious enough to have done anything but, luckily for the Doctor, the control room door slid open and the Deputy burst in looking agitated. He was speaking before he was fully through the door.

'Report from Floor 109, Chief. Two of the oldsters have apparently disappeared and it is believed that they have gone down the XY3 standard issue waste disposal unit.'

'What!' The Chief was genuinely thrown off-balance.

'It's unheard of, Chief,' continued the Deputy. 'I should remind you that under the emergency regulation number 56 subsection –'

'Yes, yes, I know,' the Chief cut him off impatiently. 'I have

87

to go and find out what's happened. Why do things like this always happen at the most inconvenient moment?' He started to move decisively towards the door. 'Deputy, I leave you in charge.' His face twisted into an ugly smile. 'I don't need to remind you of the consequences of any second mistake.'

'No, Chief.' The Deputy shuffled uncomfortably. And then, just as he was leaving, the Chief had a sudden inspiration. He turned back and glanced at the Doctor, who was still seated where the Regulation 13 Appendix 2 Final Conversation had taken place.

'Perhaps we should allow the Great Architect to see a copy of the Illustrated Prospectus to Paradise Towers. Might bring back happy memories.' The ugly grin returned, a relish of revenge for the discomfort the Doctor had caused him. 'Not that I shall be away long. It's against my principles to keep *anyone* waiting.'

The door slid to and he was gone.

'And no funny business with the rule book this time, all right?' The Deputy's tone was almost pleading as he had once again to assume control of the prisoner.

But the Doctor did not answer. Indeed he barely heard what the Deputy was saying. His mind was elsewhere, turning over far bigger and more baffling problems than how he was to escape again. The chat with the Chief had started to open up extraordinary possibilities but their implication still eluded him.

Perhaps the Illustrated Prospectus to the Towers would furnish the clue he still needed.

8

The Illustrated Prospectus

It was inevitable, Mel supposed, but it was still a shock. She had decided to make a detour to where they had left the TARDIS on the corner of Fountain of Happiness Square. It had seemed a good idea to be able to fix in her mind where it was located for when the time came to leave Paradise Towers. She could even mark it on Tilda and Tabby's map. Now she rather wished she hadn't bothered. The sight of the TARDIS covered all over with graffiti was not encouraging.

'Kang wallscrawl,' Pex announced, rather unnecessarily.

'I know,' Mel returned pointedly. Lots of it. As if the Blue Kangs had had a go first and then the Red Kangs had come and gone one better. There was certainly a mass of different slogans, paintings and signs covering the familiar blue telephone box. The Doctor, Mel feared, was not going to be too pleased.

'Quiet!' Pex had tensed suddenly and his eyes were scanning the dark corners of the Square.

'What is it now?' Mel enquired patiently.

'I thought I saw a Blue Kang.'

'Relax!' Mel urged him. 'I know the Blue Kangs weren't very nice to you but if you're going to be this jumpy all the time it's going to be hopeless.'

'You don't know them like I do,' Pex insisted. But Mel had already started to leave the Square. It was no good crying over spilt milk. Hopefully, there would be time at a later date to clean up the TARDIS. For the moment they had to get on.

Sometimes when you're in a hurry or slightly flustered, you don't trust your instincts. Mel was anxious to pull Pex out of his panic so she didn't perhaps pay enough attention to hers.

Because, as they left the Square, Mel had a very strong sense that they were being followed. And not by Blue Kangs.

'Welcome one and all to Paradise Towers, which will be your new home for a good few years to come . . .'

The Doctor settled back comfortably in anticipation. The Illustrated Prospectus promised well from the point of view of information. After all, it was intended to help future inhabitants not lure unsuspecting tourists like the aged video-brochure that had so impressed Mel.

'Some of you will understandably feel nervous at leaving everything you know for a strange new environment . . .' The voice was jolly and reassuring, the music that accompanied it bland and up-beat. The Doctor found it all rather creepy.

'However, we believe once you've tasted the Paradise Towers experience you won't want to change it for any other . . .' Well, it's not an experience *like* any other, the Doctor agreed mentally but personally he'd have exchanged it for a weekend locked in a hotel room with the Daleks.

Pictures of various aspects of Paradise Towers started to appear now. And the Doctor realised that, in the original concept, it was not just the swimming pool that was planned on such a lavish and spacious scale. The video-brochure had not lied. Now he had walked round the desolate streets, the Doctor found he could recognise places he had passed through in their gleaming new counterparts on the screen.

'Our motto,' intoned the voice, 'is "Build High for Happiness" . . .'

So there was one less mystery. The Kangs' code phrase that had puzzled him before was the slogan the inhabitants had been given when they first arrived, one no doubt intended to give them confidence and pride in the soaring Towers. The Kangs, he was sure, knew nothing of that. For them it was simply a resonant phrase, a magic conjuration against disaster.

'The facilities of this mighty structure are unrivalled,' the cheery voice continued as glossy image followed glossy image. 'Every care has been taken to ensure that Paradise Towers will not only be thoroughly enjoyable but also safe and clean . . .'

There was a great deal of din in the background behind the Doctor but he was so tense with concentration that he tried to filter the noise out and hear only what was on the screen.

'Paradise Towers has been specially designed for you by . . .'

The Doctor leant forward eagerly but it was impossible to hear a word of what was being said on the screen. The noise in the control room was quite deafening. As if somebody had decided to move all the furniture around and somebody else was trying to stop them.

The Doctor turned. 'Will you please keep quiet, I'm –' He stopped in mid-sentence as he finally realised the explanation for all the upheaval. The Deputy and other Caretakers guarding the Doctor were on the floor, arms tied behind their backs and gags in their mouths. And over them, crossbows in hand, stood a small group of Red Kangs with Bin Liner and Fire Escape at their head.

'How you do, Doctor?' Bin Liner, grinning, gave the Doctor the Kang salute. With delight the Doctor returned it.

'Bin Liner! Fire Escape! How did you get here?'

'We track you down the carrydoors,' Fire Escape answered, 'creep in when the Chief Caretaker left and bundle up these others.' She gestured to the woe-begone Caretakers on the floor.

'Sorry to disturb you,' apologised Bin Liner, in whose hand a copy of the small square key card was visible, spoils no doubt from an unwary Caretaker.

'Not at all,' the Doctor replied. 'I'm delighted to see you. You must have taken quite a risk.'

'You took a risk for us,' Fire Escape returned simply. 'But we must all leave now, Doctor.' She placed the key card in position and the door started to open.

'Of course,' the Doctor agreed eagerly. 'There's bound to be an alarm system that the Deputy can set off given half a chance.'

He was halfway across the control room when he remembered the Prospectus was still playing. 'How stupid of me,' the Doctor muttered. He rushed back to the screen and removed from it the high tech disc within that contained the Prospectus. Crucial evidence to be examined in more detail later.

As he stepped over the recumbent Deputy, he waved the disc cheerily at him. 'I'm sure there are rules to govern all this, aren't there, Deputy?'

Gagged as he was, the furious Deputy could only mumble indistinctly.

'You know,' the Doctor remarked as they left the Headquarters, 'that's the most intelligent thing he's said so far.'

The door slid shut behind them leaving the Deputy to face the wrath of his Chief for a second time.

The Chief Caretaker peered down the XY3 standard issue waste disposal unit but there were certainly no traces of Tilda and Tabby for him to see. He had a pretty shrewd idea where they would end up, of course, but it worried him that once again *he* had not given any orders. Someone else had sucked them down to their fate. Someone or something. He would have to investigate very closely. For the moment, however, he had a more immediate task: to comfort the agitated Maddy, who hovered by his side, her plump face a picture of puzzlement and distress. It was she who had summoned the Caretakers after hearing strange noises and reported Tilda and Tabby's probable fate.

'Well, I can't think of any other explanation,' she insisted to the Chief. 'Can you?'

'Since you ask,' he returned loftily, 'thousands.'

'But it's never happened before,' Maddy persisted.

The Chief Caretaker straightened up from his investigation and gave Maddy the full force of his most disarming smile. 'You wouldn't by any chance have eaten them, would you?'

'What do you mean?' Maddy stared at him in total shock.

'I've heard rumours that such things go on, you know,' the Chief continued.

'The very idea!' Maddy exclaimed indignantly. 'They were my friends, my closest neighbours. Would I have summoned you if I'd done something wrong?'

'It was just a thought.' The Chief was pacific now. It had been worth a try but the woman was clearly an innocent, trusting fool. The real culprit was elsewhere. 'Anyway,' he assured her charmingly, 'there is no cause for panic.'

'No cause for panic!' Maddy could not believe her ears and repeated the words in disbelief. 'No cause for panic! Two of my next-door neighbours have just disappeared down the waste disposal chute!' She remembered then Tilda and Tabby's many little meannesses and acts of unfriendliness but also the awfulness of their fate. 'I wouldn't wish that on anybody.'

The Chief resumed his official face. 'There will, of course, be a frank and full review of the circumstances and in due course a report will be issued to all Residents. And you can rest assured there will be no cover-up.' He repeated the last words more impressively to emphasise them. 'No cover-up at all.'

Maddy's face, however, was still filled with doubt. The Chief brought his face closer to hers and hissed in confidential tones. 'I would urge you, nevertheless, for the moment to keep the matter quiet. We don't want to alarm people unduly, do we?'

'Well,' Maddy hesitated, 'I'm not really sure that I ought to.'

Fuller measures were going to be needed and the Chief, suppressing his impatience, re-assumed his official voice. 'Not that I would in any way wish to bribe you to hold your tongue but rules could be made flexible and it could be arranged for you to move into this flat instead of your own. It is, after all, substantially larger.' His eyes invited Maddy to take in the attractiveness of the move into this bright snug apartment. 'After all, what's the good of panicking people when, I repeat, everything is under control?'

Maddy regarded the flat longingly. Her desire for it battled with her innate honesty and, for the moment at least, won.

'Well,' she conceded slowly, 'I would hate to upset anybody.'

'Exactly.' The Chief allowed himself a smile. The fool had taken the bait and would keep her tongue for the moment. Whether she would actually get the promised flat or not would depend on later developments. 'And now if you'll excuse me,' he continued charmingly. 'I think I will depart to begin my investigation.' He paused as if in thought. 'In the Basement, perhaps, might be the best place.'

The Chief left almost immediately. His exterior was still calm, a mask of efficiency and tact, but underneath, his brain was seething with questions. The feeling of unease was back with a vengeance now and there was nothing he could do to dispel it. He would have to confront his pet in the Basement. Tilda and Tabby were not part of the diet he had planned. Daddy was going to have to be very strict indeed with his darling.

Maddy said her goodbyes to the Chief with appropriate deference and then watched him walk away down the street. The flat was tempting but she was not at all sure she should take it. Nor was she convinced that she should hold her tongue. Rezzie gossip had told her about Caretakers being killed. Now Rezzies themselves were threatened. And Tilda and Tabby had been the toughest and most self-reliant of them all, eating good fresh meat long after the rest had given up hope of finding it. If she didn't speak out, who was going to go next? She went home to ponder with a heavy heart.

Mel had not quite shaken off the feeling of being followed – even though they had been travelling for some time now without sight of anything, despite Pex's nervous staring about at every crossroads. The map, meanwhile, was proving an incalculable boon. They were making good progress and Mel had even located a lift that, if it worked, would take them right to the top of the Towers. It was on the 48th floor and they were nearly there now.

As it came into view, Pex started to go towards it to investigate. Mel gently restrained him. After their previous experience with a lift she preferred to do the checking herself.

A careful glance round the nearby street corners and up the nearest staircases assured her no one was there. 'Come on,' she beckoned to Pex, 'it's all safe. Quick!'

She entered the confined space and Pex reluctantly followed. The interior certainly boded well. It was comparatively free of wallscrawl and the control panel seemed undamaged. The floor indicator was even reading the right floor number, '48', which was the first time Mel had ever come across that in the Towers.

'Now all I have to do is press the button for the 304th floor and –'

'Er, Mel –' Pex sounded uneasy but that was perfectly normal for him so Mel ignored his interruption and confidently pressed the button. Unfortunately, nothing happened.

'Mel – look!' Pex's voice was sounding really scared now. Scared enough for Mel to notice and follow the line of his pointing finger.

Down the street towards them came a large, white, wheeled robot with headlights gleaming in the gloom. It made a soft regular whirring sound. And on its front a ferocious-looking corkscrew device turned menacingly. Mel gasped. Was this what had been following them all that time? It was scary in a way pursuing Kangs would never be and she felt her heart thump.

'What is it, Pex?'

'I'll explain later,' Pex urged plaintively. 'Could you just press the button?'

Mel had no more wish to stay around and face the robot than Pex so she pressed the button again. Nothing happened. The door stayed open and the robot, corkscrew rotating, came nearer. If the lift failed to move, they were trapped.

Mel pressed the button yet again. There was a faint whirring sound and then, after an agonising pause, the lift doors slid shut and the lift was in motion, leaving the robot behind.

'You see, we call those Cleaners,' Pex began to explain, 'and sometimes they –'

'Pex!' Mel was eager to hear his explanation but she had noticed something that took priority. She pointed to the lift indicator.

'Am I imagining things?'

'Why?'

'Are we going up – or are we going down?'

Pex thought for a moment. The indicator certainly showed them going down but that wasn't necessarily a true sign of what was happening. But Pex quickly decided that, for once, the indicator was telling the truth. 'We're going down,' he admitted.

'But I pressed the button to go up,' Mel protested.

Pex nodded ruefully. 'But the Kangs play a game, you see. These lifts only take one instruction at a time. So the Kangs get in and press the button for all kinds of floors up and down the building and the lift will have to go to all those floors before it'll get to the floor we want to go.'

Mel listened, horror-struck. 'So we could be stuck in here going up and down for hours?'

Pex nodded.

'And we could end up facing that dreadful Cleaner thing again – or something worse?'

Pex nodded again. 'Now do you see why I don't like travelling in lifts?'

Mel had to acknowledge that she did see why. And she had thought they were doing so well in their trek to the 304th floor.

'Well, Red Kangs, I have to say I'd never imagined I'd be glad to see this place again.' The Doctor took in the familiar details of the Brainquarters and was surprised by how comforting it seemed now after the lair of the Chief Caretaker. The Kangs were sometimes difficult and unpredictable but they were not mad, bad or totally ruthless. That meant a lot in Paradise Towers.

'Be seated, Doctor,' Bin Liner invited.

'And drink.' Fire Escape produced a can of Fizzade from the machine and pulled off the metal tag. The Doctor and the other Red Kangs laughed at the reminder of their last encounter as they all settled down to talk.

'Thank you, Fire Escape.' The Doctor graciously accepted the can and thankfully downed half of it. While the rest were being served, however, he felt he had to press on. 'Before we doing anything else,' he told his hosts, 'we must look at the Illustrated Prospectus.' He reached in his pocket to pull it out but it was the wrong pocket. Quite a few pockets later, however, the Doctor finally brought the precious disc to light.

'You do have something we can look at it on, I presume?' the Doctor enquired.

Fire Escape pointed nonchalantly to what looked like a large fire extinguisher with a screen fitted to its top.

'Ah, the wonders of Paradise Towers technology,' the Doctor muttered to himself. It appeared to be junk but the Doctor had sufficient confidence now in the Kangs to believe it would work every bit as well as the talkiphones.

Setting up the Picturespout, as the Kangs called it, took a little time, and, while Bin Liner worked at this, the others huddled round the Doctor, eager to ask questions of this strange being who had entered their enclosed world.

'Is it true that there are other places, not like the Towers?'

'Oh yes,' the Doctor replied. 'Many other places. More than you could count if you started counting now and went on until you were unalive. All with different languages and different clothes and different customs.'

'Do they all have Rezzies who eat Kangs?'

The Doctor shook his head.

'But Kangs,' one of the smaller Reds protested, 'they all have Kangs, don't they?'

The Doctor shook his head again. 'No. No Kangs. No Red Kangs. No Blue Kangs. No any-colour Kangs.'

'No Kangs.' Fire Escape repeated the words wonderingly and the Kangs looked at each other in surprise. That there were other worlds had never occured to them but then nobody had ever attempted to explain the facts before. That these worlds operated on different principles from the rules of the

Kang game and the harsh facts of survival in Paradise Towers amazed them. And gave them much to think about and discuss in the days to come.

'We want you to tell us about such places.'

The Doctor was happy to agree but at that moment Bin Liner announced that the Picturespout was 'all shape-ship and ready' and they could view the Prospectus. They all realised that delightful though it was to talk of other places, their immediate concern was the state of the Towers.

Everyone shifted on the floor until they had a good view and the Picturespout went into action. The opening images were already familiar to the Doctor but they so fascinated the Kangs, who had never seen pictures of the Towers as it was first completed, that he did not have the heart to hurry on through. At last, however, they came to the part of the Prospectus he had been studying when the Kangs had rescued him. The cheery voice framed that tantalising sentence and this time he was going to hear all of it.

'Paradise Towers,' the voice announced, 'has been specially designed for you by Kroagnon, universally known as the Great Architect, the genius responsible for Golden Dream Park, the Bridge of Perpetual Motion, Miracle City . . .'

'Miracle City!' The Doctor's eyes were agleam. A name had finally jogged his momory and the whole thing was suddenly falling into place. The name Kroagnon on the coin. The Great Architect never seen since the Towers were built. And now a list of his achievements had mentioned Miracle City. The Doctor knew all about Miracle City and he intended that the Kangs should know the whole story too.

The indicator said Mel and Pex were going up now. So far they had stopped at the 9th floor, the 102nd floor, the 56th floor, the 239th floor, the 9th floor (again) and the 173rd floor but the doors had not opened on anything alarming like a Cleaner waiting outside and they had always shut to order.

'Well, I suppose it is one way of seeing Paradise Towers,' Mel announced philosophically, now that Pex had fully informed her of the dangers of Cleaners and Caretakers. 'Just so long as nothing goes wrong with the lift.'

At that moment the lights inside the lift started to flicker and then the whole lift started to judder alarmingly. Pex was immediately on edge. 'What did you say?' he asked, too nervous to really listen.

'It doesn't matter really,' Mel replied, still trying to make the best of the situation. 'Unless, of course, the lift sticks completely between floors.'

She should have known better. The lift promptly juddered to a complete halt, stuck between floors.

'Well, at least the lights haven't gone out,' Mel insisted brightly.

Then the lights went out too. They were stuck there in the blackness unable to get out or summon help. They couldn't even tell which floors they were stuck between. It was too much for Pex.

'I hate the dark,' he whimpered quietly.

To be honest, Mel wasn't too keen on it either. And it was fortunate for both of them that a small red emergency light now came on, allowing them to see just a little in the semi-darkness. Both of them started to feel around for the control panel. It was Mel who found it first.

'The controls are really stiff, though,' she panted, trying to get them to work. Something had clearly jammed and she made no impression at all.

'Here. Let me.' Pex may not have been the braver of the two but he was undoubtedly the stronger and Mel pulled back as far as she could in the confined space in the lift to let him get to the control panel.

In the flickering red light, Mel saw Pex go through the same extraordinary preparatory routine he had used when he bent the street lamp. It seemed like that had happened days ago but she realised with a shock it was probably only a matter of hours. But here again was the same flexing and the same deep breathing. And then Pex came right up to the control panel and brought the whole force of his hand down on it with a strange war-like cry.

They waited for a moment and then the main light came on. It was a hopeful sign.

'Well done, Pex!' Mel exclaimed. In the full light she could see he was looking pleased with himself, and, for once, she did not begrudge him his complacency. And a moment later the lift mercifully juddered back into action.

The floor indicator, however, started to go crazy and Mel had a tremendous sinking feeling in her stomach. 'The only snag is,' she called to Pex over the juddering, 'that we seem to be going down. Very fast.'

And indeed the lift was all too obviously plummeting down the floors of the Towers at a phenomenal rate. Neither of them cared to discuss when and where the lift would come to a halt.

The Chief was walking along the 48th floor on his way to the Basement when he saw it. A Megapodic Mark 7Z Cleaner standing by one of the few functional lifts with its corkscrew attachment in action.

'What are you doing here, Robotic Cleaner 479?' he demanded as he came up and could see the registration mark on its side. 'I didn't order you to stand there. Get back to the 67Y Depot at once.'

The Cleaner did not move.

'Do you hear my orders?' the Chief barked. It was the first time he had faced an insubordinate Cleaner although reason told him that they had to exist for all the unauthorised killings to have taken place. But he felt certain a little firm handling would soon put matters to rights.

It didn't. Instead Robotic Cleaner 479 did something totally unexpected. It turned to face him and then started to force him back down the corridor. Its corkscrew rotated so ferociously that the Chief did not feel like confronting it directly. Instead he was forced to employ gentler means.

'What's going on, Robotic Cleaner 479?' he asked plaintively as he was edged back down the corridor. 'Look, there's no need for this. Really there isn't.'

And then the ghastly truth of what was happening struck him. He wasn't any longer going down to the Basement to see his pet under his own steam, choosing his own time and his own route. He was being forced to go there by some greater power.

The Doctor had the total attention of the Red Kangs as he talked. It would have been possible to hear a pin drop. And no wonder. He was telling them how the world in which they had lived all their lives came into being.

'Kroagnon,' the Doctor was saying, 'was a brilliant architect who created a number of projects around the Galaxy. But, for all his brilliance, a lot of people didn't trust him. Miracle City was his masterpiece. But the architect showed a great reluctance to finish the building and move out so that the people could move in. He thought they'd spoil the beauty of his creation. They got him out in the end, of course, but the people who moved in lived to regret it.'

Fire Escape gasped. 'He made them unalive?'

'Faults occurred and lives were lost,' the Doctor answered, 'but his responsibility could never be proved so he got away with it. There were many who believed it was some sort of revenge for not being allowed to have his own way.'

The Doctor took a deep breath and pursed his lips. 'But, you see, my dear Kangs, space is a big place. And he *was* brilliant and so he got other work including, of course, Paradise Towers.'

'Blank walls and cleaners!' It was an exclamation the Doctor had not heard before. But it was apparently the only one strong enough to express Bin Liner's feelings at the implications of what the Doctor had said.

'Of course,' the Doctor continued gravely, 'after that, he disappeared. The Chief Caretaker told me that. But mayhaps, my dear Red Kangs –' he paused to take in their anxious and intent faces. 'Mayhaps your parents thought they were being clever by leaving him here trapped in some way in his own building. Perhaps to guard its secret. Perhaps to stop him

101

capping it with a greater project. Most likely to prevent the sort of problems there had been over Miracle City.'

The Doctor paused again, the gravity of what he was saying having an effect on him too. 'But if your parents did do that,' he then concluded, 'they did a very foolish thing. Because, no matter how deep they buried him in Paradise Towers, he's bound to get out in the end.'

There was a long silence. Bin Liner broke it.

'What must Red Kangs do, Doctor?'

'We'll fight for you,' Fire Escape added. And there was immediately a chorus of other offers to fight.

The Doctor held up his hand gently. 'You must do something more difficult than that. You must tell me all you know.' His eyes met Bin Liner's. 'I mean, that door with the smoke coming out of it. Where is it?'

Bin Liner hesitated. 'Please,' the Doctor insisted, 'it's important.'

'In the Basement,' Bin Liner admitted. 'The Cleaners have a secret alleviator. Red Kangs have used it and seen –'

'And seen what?'

'Things they could not speak of,' Bin Liner mumbled shamefacedly.

The Doctor decided it was again time to take action. The Kangs too were happier with that than providing explanations. 'I'm going down to the Basement to find out what's going on,' he announced. 'I'm sure for a start that the Chief Caretaker knows a lot more than he's letting on.'

'I'll go outlook with you, Doctor,' Bin Liner immediately put in, delighted the conversation had taken this turn.

'And me,' put in Fire Escape eagerly. Again there was a babble of voices offering help.

The Doctor held up his hand once more to command silence. 'All right, all right. Bin Liner and Fire Escape, you come with me. I'm sure there'll be work for the rest of you to do in time. Stay here for the moment though. The three of us must go immediately.'

'No!' It was the voice of the Blue Kang leader. She and the rest of her Kangs were massed at the top of the narrow stairs and were pouring down now, crossbows in hand. So intent had been the Red Kangs on the Doctor's story that they had been able to force an entry upstairs without being noticed.

The Blue Kang leader was triumphant. 'Red Kangs leave no outlooks,' she jeered. 'Blue Kangs have got into their Brainquarters and won the game. Blue Kangs are best!'

'Blue Kangs are best! Blue Kangs are best!' the others joined in with victorious pride. Not surprisingly, perhaps, a counter cry of 'Red Kangs are best!' went up from the ambushed.

The quarrelling was deafening and the Doctor had to raise his voice to a shout to make himself heard. 'Please!' he cried when some semblance of quiet had been created. 'The future of Paradise Towers is at stake. We all have to work together.' He turned to the Blue Kang leader. 'You have got to help us.'

It took precious minutes for the Blue Kangs to calm down and listen. They were so excited by their victory that at first they could not take in what the Doctor was saying. But eventually they grasped its import.

'Look,' urged the Doctor, 'you've got to believe me. I'm sure the Red Kangs will agree that you've won this round of the game. But there won't be any games worth playing if we don't discover who's been ordering the killings. Will you let us go to the Basement?'

'More,' the Blue Kang returned, convinced at last. 'I will go with you.'

'Good,' the Doctor said approvingly. 'Then you'll see with your own eyes what's going on.'

'Blue Kang Eye-Spy saw the Chief Caretaker footing it there too,' the leader added, indicating one of the others, who nodded agreement.

'Then we must hurry.' The Doctor turned back to Bin Liner. 'What's the quickest way to get there?'

'We must use the Cleaners' secret alleviator,' Bin Liner replied.

'Excellent.' The Doctor and his three companions turned

to say farewell to the rest of the Blue and Red Kangs gathered together in one space for the first time in their young lives.

'Build High for Happiness!'

'Build High for Happiness!' came the answer of the other Kangs as they made the Kang salute.

Build High for Happiness, indeed, the Doctor thought as they hurried away from the Brainquarters. But, let us hope, not Dig Deep for Disaster.

9

The Basement

'Where are we now?' Mel asked. The lift had finally stopped
its dizzying descent and she and Pex waited anxiously for
developments.

The door slid open. To Mel the exterior seemed pitch-black.
Pex, however, had barely poked his head out before his square
jaw dropped in dismay. 'Oh no,' he murmured.

'What is it?'

Pex gulped. 'I think we're in the Basement.'

'As in "Forbidden to all Residents of Paradise Towers on
Pain of Death"?'

Pex nodded. The horror of their situation rendered them
both speechless. They peered out in the blackness together
and, as she looked, Mel's eyes became accustomed to the
gloom and she could just about make out a long dark corridor.
Then beyond it, huge studded doors. Worse still, she then
perceived in the distance white-bodied Cleaners coming and
going with trailers at their back. One approached the studded
doors and they flew open to receive it. Smoke billowed out and
then a huge mechanical roar echoed through the whole
basement. At least Mel thought at first it was mechanical.
Then, maybe because of her overwrought state, she started to
think that the roar was really a voice.

'Soon . . . soon . . . soon I shall be free . . .'

That was what Mel thought she could make out. But she
couldn't be sure. The whole atmosphere with the smoke, the
dank corridors and the Cleaners shooting hither and thither
was alarming enough without indulging in fantasies.

'We have to get out of here,' she hissed to Pex. 'It's only a matter of time before those Cleaners notice us.' She frantically tried the lift-control button. 'This thing is really jammed this time.'

'Shall I hit it?' Pex was already preparing himself mentally for another of his powerful blows. The physical preparations were about to follow. There was, of course, a very real possibility that this time Pex would break the control completely and they would be stuck here for good. Or until the Cleaners picked them off. But Mel also realised there was no real practical alternative to trying and so nothing to lose. She nodded her agreement for Pex to proceed.

'Soon I shall be free . . . soon. . .' the eerie voice still echoed down the corridor as Pex prepared.

For a moment she thought his nerve and his strength would fail him. But Pex lunged at the control button with even greater force than before and dealt it a savage and sudden blow. There was an ominous pinging sound and she thought he had merely succeeded in breaking it. The lights flickered ominously.

And then she knew instinctively before it happened that they were going to be all right. The lights steadied and the door shut, cutting out the mechanical roaring and the smoke-filled corridor. And there was even better news. The lift was clearly going up the building now. Very fast.

'Chief . . . Chief . . . Chief . . . '

The Deputy Chief had managed to get free with the aid of some of the other Caretakers returning from duty on the streets of the Towers. But getting free now seemed to have been the least of his problems. His next worry was how to tell the Chief what had happened without undergoing the 327 Appendix 3 Subsection 9 Death himself. A less loyal or less stupid man might have delayed informing the Chief but the Deputy was trained to report to his superior immediately. Which led to a third problem that made the other two pale into insignificance. Finding the Chief.

It was quite without precedent and quite without

106

explanation. No amount of running through the rule book could yield him a possible solution. However hard and however long the Deputy tried to contact the Chief via his Mark 12 LDCE all he received back was total silence.

The Deputy called out the Chief's name until his voice was hoarse. But there was no getting round the dreadful fact. The Chief could not be contacted. And the Deputy had no inkling of his whereabouts.

Put more simply and more frighteningly, the Chief had disappeared.

At that very moment the Chief, flanked by insistent Megapodic Cleaners, was confronting through billowing smoke the two fiery red unblinking eyes of his pet. The eyes burned with a fervour that made the Chief's blood run cold but he tried to put a brave face on it.

'Look,' he began, blusteringly, 'I don't understand what the matter is, my beauty. I've always made sure you've had lots of little tender morsels to make you big and strong. So why have you been giving my Cleaners orders that aren't my orders and killing people I didn't tell you to kill?'

There was no denying the power of the voice that replied now. Nor could the Chief any longer doubt that its mechanical rumblings framed words and words that showed the workings of a powerful mind.

'The bodies the Cleaners brought were not right!' the voice boomed.

'Not right?' the Chief queried, a tremor in his voice he could not conceal. 'What for?'

'For me to live in!'

The power and energy of the reply almost knocked the Chief off his feet but he managed to just about keep his balance. 'To live in? I don't understand.'

'Neither could they,' the voice replied, with withering contempt. 'That was the problem.'

The Doctor and his three Kang companions heard this last exchange as they crept stealthily out of the Service lift and into the corridor. They were still breathing heavily from their frantic descent and the gloom of their surroundings immediately oppressed their spirits. But they had to persist. Led by the Doctor, they edged their way along the slimy corridor as near to the Chief as they dared to come without being spotted by the Cleaners.

From there, flattened against the wall, they were able to pick up the fatal last exchanges between the Chief Caretaker and his pet.

'You see, my pet,' the Chief was saying, still struggling to get control of the situation, 'all these bodies disappearing. People are beginning to notice, you know.'

'No matter.' The two words were magnificent in their dismissiveness.

'What did you say?' The Chief peered through the smoke at the eyes, horrified by what he heard and saw.

'I am ready now. I have my plan.' The eyes were brighter and redder than ever.

The Chief was babbling now, completely unnerved. 'Look . . . it's . . . it's nice to have you chattier than usual, my pet. But I do think you might be a bit more grateful for all I've done for you.'

'You have done all I need you to do.' The voice boomed through the rapidly clearing smoke. 'I need only one more thing from you.'

The Cleaners were edging the terrified Chief Caretaker through the doorway now towards the evilly glowing eyes. From his viewpoint, the Doctor could see only part of what was happening. But he could hear the roaring grow louder and louder. And see the outlines of a large pulsating machine in which the eyes were located.

'Want something, do you?' shrieked the Chief, as the Cleaners forced him relentlessly on. 'And suppose I won't give it to you?'

'You have no choice,' the voice replied. And the Doctor saw the machine start to burst apart in a horrifying explosion of energy and matter. The eyes glowed still stronger and stronger as the panel around them crumbled away.

And then a tube-like dome started to slowly descend from the ceiling of the inner sanctum. And the Chief was edged nearer and nearer until he stood underneath it totally deprived of all speech.

The voice seemed to be everywhere now. 'I am Kroagnon, the Great Architect!' it announced. 'And I will put an end to you. And everyone in Paradise Towers!'

The dome started to descend over the luckless Chief and he gave one last cry as it enveloped him. And the energy was everywhere, crackling like flashes of lightning all around the dome. Sparks shot everywhere and the stout doors themselves sizzled and buckled with the power. Then the machine and the eyes were gone. No sound came from inside the dome. And wherever Kroagnon was, he was no longer in his prison.

The studded doors banged to with a crash. The Doctor was so appalled that he was thankful not to see any more. The same was true of his companions, who stood, still mesmerised, staring at the door, their eyes seared by the image of the crumbling panel, the descending dome and their last sight of the petrified Chief.

What none of them had noticed was that the Cleaners who had guarded the Chief remained outside the doors. And now, their principal task over, they had become aware of the intruders. And two of them, their corkscrew blades whirring, were making directly for the group.

'Ware Cleaners!' called Bin Liner, the first to scent the danger.

'Quick to the lift!' the Doctor cried to the others. He gestured them to run as fast as they could but moved himself towards the Cleaners to try and delay them for a few vital seconds by battering at them with his umbrella.

'No, Doctor, wait!' Fire Escape called. The Kangs had no intention of abandoning the Doctor or gaining their safety at his expense. Instead they had their crossbows at the ready in a matter of seconds. But it was difficult for them to aim at the Cleaners while the Doctor was in the line of fire.

The Doctor's umbrella was wrenched from his grasp in the

struggle. And a moment later a grasping white claw fastened on his neck. He could feel it contracting, squeezing the breath out of him. Just my luck, he found himself thinking as he started to faint, the third time round I really have fallen for that old trick.

The Kangs fired their crossbows. They could not afford to wait for a more favourable opportunity any longer if they were to save the Doctor. And fortunately for him, their aim was true. Both Cleaners were hit by an arrow on the body which embedded itself in the metal casing and the third struck the claw that held the Doctor itself causing the grip to relax for just a moment.

'Doctor! Quick! Now!'

The Doctor summoned his last ounce of strength and pulled free of the metal claw. Abandoning his umbrella to its fate, he ran after the Kangs. The effect of the arrows was to momentarily immobilise the Cleaners but it would only be for a moment and then they would be in pursuit again.

The fleeing quartet made the Service Lift just in time. As its metal doors shut behind them, they caught a glimpse of the Cleaners already back in motion and coming after them. But for now, with the Service Lift speeding back up the Towers, they were safe. And even thankful that the Lift used by the Cleaners had been kept in working order while the rest in the Towers had been allowed to fall into disrepair.

The Doctor struggled to get his breath back.

'The Doctor really is icehot –' the Blue Kang remarked approvingly.

'Very hot,' the Doctor couldn't resist putting in as he mopped his brow.

'He's not a yawny oldster anyway,' Bin Liner agreed.

The Doctor turned to the Blue Kang leader, whose name, he had discovered, after all their adventures together, was Drinking Fountain. 'Now you understand the dangerous position we are all in. We must get all the Kangs together, not just those waiting in the Brainquarters.'

Drinking Fountain nodded. The two Red Kangs meanwhile

were trying to make sense of what they had seen.

'And is the Chief Caretaker really unalive?' Fire Escape asked the Doctor wonderingly.

The Doctor nodded thoughtfully. 'As himself, yes. But you saw what happened. So far as I can understand what was going on, up to now Kroagnon has simply been a mind without a body. Just as your parents left him when they made that fatal decision to lock him up in the Basement to stop him harming the new occupants.'

'But the sparks and the dome –' Bin Liner began, the vivid images still lodged in her brain.

'Well,' sighed the Doctor, 'I fear Kroagnon may have spent his time down there devising a means to perform corpoelectroscopy – a way of transferring his brilliant brain into some host body.'

'And what's the comeout, Doctor?' Three anxious faces peered at him in the half-light of the lift.

'I can't be certain,' the Doctor replied. His face was grim and he was not going to insult the Kangs by failing to prepare them for the worst. 'Kroagnon will undoubtedly not stay locked in his Basement much longer. He's bound to show himself – in one form or another . . . '

The studded metal doors flew open. And a figure walked stiffly out. It was the Chief and yet not the Chief. It was the Chief's face and yet the face was pale and strangely coloured with a greenish hue. It was the Chief's voice but much more mechanical sounding with a soft, steely power the Chief had never had. It was the Chief's body and yet its movements were stiff and robotic but at the same time powerful and menacing as the Chief's had never been. And, most eerie of all, it was the Chief's uniform but what was once grey and tattered had become white and glistening as if purged by some violent electrical process.

'Attention all Robotic Cleaners . . . Attention all Robotic Cleaners . . . '

The figure waited calmly as the cohorts of Cleaners

111

assembled. He had no need to hurry. All the power and all the time were on his side. It was not until the last Cleaner was in place that he began speaking in his soft, mesmeric mechanical voice.

'At last Kroagnon can leave the basement prison they trapped his bodyless brain in and return in this borrowed body to the corridors and lifts of his own creation.'

As he spoke the figure seemed to grow in strength and confidence with every word. Now there were contempt and anger behind the soft control.

'Paradise Towers has become filthy, crumbling and broken-down, a disgrace to me, the Great Architect who built it. And who is responsible for this disgusting mess?' he demanded. 'People are responsible, that is who. Dirty, untidy creatures of flesh and blood who should never have been allowed to pollute this beautiful environment.'

He advanced a few steps further and the doors that had led to the prison he had been held in for so long shut behind him with a finality that inspired him still further.

'They buried me away because I wanted to stop them using the Towers. And now it is your job to destroy them.'

His eyes, the burning red eyes of the Chief's pet not the bloodshot eyes of the Chief Caretaker himself, took in the serried ranks of Cleaners, all ready and gleaming white.

'You will destroy them,' he repeated. 'All of them!'

10

The Pool in the Sky

'Three hundred . . . three hundred and one . . . three hundred and two . . . three hundred and three . . . three hundred and . . .'

Mel held her breath. Then the lift juddered to a halt. And the floor indicator read very clearly '304'. 'We made it!' she exclaimed with relief. But what, she wondered, was in store up here at the very top of Paradise Towers? More horrors?

The lift door opened. A blindingly bright light flooded in, almost dazzling both Mel and Pex. And, at the same moment, the sound of soft, sweet recorded music hit their ears.

They advanced out of the lift almost in a trance and walked along a deep carpeted corridor decorated with potted plants and gaily coloured murals all as good as new.

'I just don't believe it,' Mel murmured. 'I really don't.'

They pushed open the beautiful glass door and there it was. The Pool in the Sky. The pool Mel had dreamed about. And, incredibly, it was exactly as it had been in the pictures Mel had seen in the video-brochure. The marble floors. The luxurious loungers. The shimmering blue water. Utterly spotless and completely deserted. And, somehow, here in reality it was even more magnificent than any pictures could have made it seem. After all Mel had been through, it seemed almost too good to be true.

The soft music wafted over them as they took in their surroundings. 'It's just the sort of pool I've dreamed of,' Mel announced, flopping down into one of the lavishly upholstered loungers that lay by its side. 'Why don't the residents of the Towers ever use it, Pex?'

Pex was pacing anxiously by the pool side. He was still unsettled despite the relaxing nature of the environment. 'We should not be here,' he kept muttering as he wandered around, peering anxiously into every crevice. 'It's the home of the unalive.'

'I think that's all nonsense,' Mel replied, lazily stretching out her arms. 'Don't you think it's wonderful to be somewhere clean and calm and relaxing?'

'It makes me nervous,' Pex replied.

'Everything makes you nervous.' Mel peered longingly into the water. 'I'm glad this is where I agreed to meet the Doctor. Aren't you going to have a swim, Pex?'

Pex shook his head and continued his searching.

'I just don't understand you, Pex. I think that all that talk about this place being dangerous is just a trick by the Caretakers so they don't have to come and clean up the pool all the time.'

Pex completed his nervy reconnaissance and having found nothing, perched unhappily on the edge of the next lounger to Mel.

'Just a few minutes to take the weight off my feet,' Mel announced, 'and then it's straight into that lovely cool water.'

She looked down again longingly into the heated water. She assumed that the bubbles she saw near the middle of the pool were something to do with the heating system. It did not occur to her that there might be anything sinister or threatening about them.

Reports were coming in to the Red Kang Brainquarters from all over the Towers. Red and Blue Eye-Spies said that the Cleaners were on the rampage, destroying whoever they found in their path without exception. The first few floors of the Towers were already empty of all humans – apart from those unlucky enough not to move up to a higher floor in time. Drinking Fountain and Bin Liner both sent out orders to their Eye-Spies to abandon their posts and return as quickly as they could to Red Kang Brainquarters.

They came as quickly as they could, some defiant, some already scared. Only Fire Escape had still to return from a difficult mission on Floor Two. But it was apparent to everyone what was happening. Kroagnon was using the Cleaners to take over the Towers floor by floor.

'Are all the Kangs here, Blue and Red?' the Doctor asked when the Brainquarters seemed full to bursting with the young warriors who had played the Kang game for so long and now had to face something much worse.

'Yes,' Drinking Fountain returned. 'Except for Fire Escape and –' She could not complete the sentence because of what she felt.

'Those who have been made unalive?' the Doctor enquired kindly, helping her to acknowledge the sense of loss. The Blue Kang leader nodded gratefully.

Fire Escape returned soon after, her young face trying hard not to show how much what she had seen had affected her. Caretakers were not safe now. Nor Rezzies. She had seen both being made unalive.

The Doctor took in the faces around him. 'Our only hope,' he insisted, 'is to make for the great pool in the sky.'

Bin Liner shook her head obstinately. 'No ballgames. No flyposts. No visitors to the pool in the sky.' She spoke for a number of the others who nodded in agreement.

'Bin Liner, listen,' the Doctor insisted gently, 'we need time to think and plan. The Cleaners will be here in no time at all at the rate they're going. The pool in the sky is the furthest place we can go.'

Bin Liner hesitated. The others too. It was hard to let go of old superstitions but they knew they had to. And they had come to trust the Doctor, who had explained so much they did not understand. The Doctor felt sure he would be able to win them over.

'Besides, you may recall,' he added, to press his advantage, 'I have to meet my very good friend, Mel, up there.' He paused and sighed. 'I can only hope she's safely there already.'

*

115

Pex had checked all the changing cubicles and both the showers several times over. But he was still uneasy and perched uneasily on the lounger staring at the water as if it was a loaded weapon. Mel, however, was having none of it, and, feeling fully rested, had decided to take the plunge.

Plunge was not perhaps the right word. The water was deliciously warm and relaxing and she felt better the moment she climbed down the poolside steps and entered it. She swam strongly out into the middle of the pool.

'The water's really lovely,' she called to Pex. 'You ought to come and join me. It'd do you the world of good and there's absolutely nothing to be frightened of.'

She spoke too soon. She had swum very close to the bubbles which she had assumed were part of the heating system. They were not. A giant yellow mechanical crab lurked there and now, sensing its opportunity, it rose from the bottom of the pool and grabbed Mel in one of its strong metal claws.

Mel screamed and struggled. To have evaded the claws of the Cleaners to be dragged underwater by this awesome creature with its snapping claws and supple, probing metal antennae was beyond her worst nightmares.

'Pex!' she called. 'Pex, help! Do something!'

Pex dithered feebly on the side of the pool. He was so terrified by what he saw now in the water that he was unable to make any practical move to help her.

'What shall I do?' he called.

'Anything,' Mel cried back as she thrashed about in the water, trying to loosen the crab's steely grip on her wrist.

Pex called for help. Even in her agony, Mel could not quite believe it. The best this supposed hero could manage was a cry for help. Not a very powerful one at that.

'Can't you think of *anything* else?' she shouted desperately.

Pex could not. Fortunately for Mel, she was a strong swimmer and somehow she managed to swim back towards the steps of the pool. The crab, however, still held on and she knew it was only a matter of moments before she went under. Its other claw snapped ferociously around her. She could think of only one solution. Pex's gun. If he would not use it – and she had never seen him dare – she would have to use it herself.

'Quick!' she cried, edging herself nearer and nearer to the poolside steps above which Pex panicked ineffectually. 'Give me the gun! Quick!'

Pex still seemed incapable of action. Mel's strength was going and she knew the crab would soon have won their deadly tug of war. 'Come on, Pex!'

The desperation in Mel's voice finally galvanised Pex into action. He edged timidly nearer the water's edge and passed her his powerful gun. Mel grabbed it thankfully with her free hand.

It was some time before she could take aim. The crab was constantly in movement and its grip relentless. Pex, anticipating the explosion, put his fingers to his ears. And then the moment came.

Mel pulled the trigger and fired directly into the body of the crab. There was a hissing as if air was escaping. The crab's grip loosened, the body deflated and the mechanical monster sank leadenly to the bottom of the pool.

Mel stared as it sank, breathless with her struggle, wordless with relief. Pex unblocked his ears and he too watched the crab's final moments.

'Well,' he sighed, his face a picture of relief, 'I did warn you.'

Perhaps it was as well that Mel did not have the breath to reply.

It was becoming clearer and clearer to the Deputy Chief that everything was going seriously out of control. Terrifying reports were reaching him from Caretakers all over the Towers. The Cleaners were running amok all the way up to the eleventh floor and there was still no sign whatsoever of the Chief. Rules and regulations he had built his life on now seemed totally irrelevant to this alarming new situation.

The Deputy Chief was not noted for his initiative and so he puzzled hard and long about what to do. And finally he made a momentous decision, one that he had thought he would never have to make. He went to the control panel and gave out a message that would be heard by Caretakers all over the Towers on their Mark 12 LDCEs.

'Attention all Caretakers . . . Attention all Caretakers . . .'

The Deputy cleared his throat nervously and then began. 'Regulation ZZZ is now in operation. This over-rides all other rules and regulations. I repeat. This over-rides all other rules and regulations. All Caretakers are to act with extreme caution and get back here as fast as they can.'

He had been doing so well up to now but the enormity of what was happening finally struck him. 'Get back as fast as you can!' he begged frantically.

And then he sat to wait until his companions all returned. He had played the master card, the final rule of rules in his treasured book. Regulation ZZZ was in force. The main problem was that he had not the least idea what to do next.

Mel lay exhausted on her lounger. Her clothes were dry now but in her mind she was still being attacked by yellow claws. Pex beside her hung his head miserably, all too conscious of his failure. And yet, Mel realised, though he had not been brave, he had been right. He had suspected a trap in the water and she, pig-headedly, had brushed his fears aside and gone in. As if anything in Paradise Towers could be without some danger attached to it. She no longer felt let down by him now and felt she should say so. She gently put her arm on Pex's.

'Pex –' she began.

'What?'

'I'm sorry, really I am.' Mel patted his arm reassuringly. 'I do understand now why people don't dare to come here. You were right about that.'

And then a rustling sound came from one of the curtained changing cubicles at the far end of the pool. Pex tensed. They both listened again. The rustling was faint but it was unmistakable.

'It's definitely coming from over there.' Mel pointed to the offending cubicle.

118

'But I only checked it a few minutes ago,' Pex protested. Now there was potential danger there, he was no longer keen to take another look.

'Shall I go then?' Mel offered.

'If you want,' Pex agreed, with evident relief.

Mel got up wearily and walked round the pool towards the cubicle. The curtain shook slightly. Perhaps it was just the wind making the curtain move. But in the artificially controlled atmosphere of the pool there didn't seem likely to be much breeze.

Mel took a deep breath and pulled back the curtain. There was nothing there. She breathed a sigh of relief and pulled the curtain to again. She'd had quite enough surprises for one day.

'Are you sure there's nothing there?' Pex called timidly.

'Of course,' Mel replied. 'Look.' And she pulled back the curtain once more. It was Pex's stare of disbelief that first told her there *was* someone there. And then she turned and saw it was none other than the Doctor himself. It seemed too good to be true.

'Sorry to give you such a shock, Mel,' the Doctor apologised. 'This is where the Cleaners' service lift appears to come out.' The Doctor gestured and behind him Mel saw a group of Red and Blue Kangs. And behind them she could just make out the outlines of a lift door in the apparently solid tiling of the cubicle.

But how the Doctor had got there was secondary. The main thing was that he had arrived. Mel hugged him warmly. 'Oh, Doctor,' she cried, 'it's so good to see you.'

'And you, Mel,' the Doctor returned enthusiastically, 'and you.'

How long had it been since the two travellers had been separated in Fountain of Happiness Square? Neither of them was any longer quite sure. They were just delighted to be together again. Mel had so much to tell the Doctor but she sensed from the presence of the Kangs that, for all his warmth and delight at seeing her again, the Doctor had much to relate and much that had to be discussed.

The Service Lift had gone down again to bring up more of the Kangs. That the Doctor and the Kangs now got on so well was one of the things Mel wanted to know about. But she knew immediately they were united by some common danger.

If a killer crab lurked in the beautiful waters of the pool, what horrors might lurk elsewhere in the Towers?

The Chief who was not the Chief strode confidently down the streets of the 33rd floor. Progress was easy so far. The Cleaners sprayed their noxious gas and the inhabitants of the Towers fell like flies. The Caretakers were the easiest to trap since obedience was engrained in them. Caretaker number 49 stroke 7 subsection 5, for example, could easily have escaped the killer fumes. But a few words of command from his Chief, albeit strangely unlike his usual self, and Caretaker number 49 stroke 7 subsection 5 stayed docilely to choke to death in the Cleaners' spray. Well, so he should have done. Everybody had a duty to make sure Paradise Towers was made *thoroughly* clean, didn't they?

The demented progress of the released Great Architect continued. Kangs and Rezzies were sharper and evaded the Cleaners more easily but they were only escaping now to be trapped later on. And in the meantime Kroagnon urged his Cleaners to search hard and ever harder. All the nasty human beings, the Caretakers, the Residents, the Kangs were to be brought out and destroyed.

Another Caretaker collapsed, coughing, across his path. Kroagnon looked down fastidiously as the unlucky victim expired. And then he stepped over the corpse and carried on down the street with the Cleaners in his wake. He didn't really like leaving bodies littering the streets. But the Cleaners could come back to collect the rubbish later.

For in the meantime the Chief who was once the Chief had a pressing visit to make. To the Caretakers' Headquarters. From there he would be able to plan his whole campaign with even more deadly efficiency backed by the screens and maps 'his' former control room contained.

The Deputy rose to his feet as the figure entered. His immediate feeling was one of relief. The Chief who had been lost had returned and he no longer had to take on the awesome responsibilities of Regulation ZZZ. But as the Chief walked stiffly into the room, the oddness of his appearance stopped the Deputy in his tracks. The presence of a pair of Cleaners in his wake added to the Deputy's growing sense of unease.

'The Towers have become appallingly dirty,' the Chief announced, brushing aside the Deputy's attempted welcoming speech.

'Sorry, Chief,' the Deputy returned meekly. 'We do our best with all that wallscrawl as you know and we try to make the Rezzies throw everything down the waste disposal chutes and—'

'That is not what I mean,' the Chief snapped back. And the Deputy noticed how mechanical and yet threatening his voice sounded. 'The whole place is polluted with flesh. Living flesh. We must remove it all. I have returned to take charge of operations.'

The Deputy had received some odd orders in his time but this was beyond anything in the rule book that he had ever come across. He gulped, unable to believe the grisliness of what he heard. 'Flesh?' he repeated weakly. 'You did say living flesh?'

'Oh yes.' The red eyes flickered dangerously now and the Deputy felt they were unlike any eyes he had seen before. He tried to protest but his protests were ignored.

'I believe, Deputy Chief,' the strange voice continued, 'there is a rule book and the rule book says in Rule One, Paragraph One, Section One, that the orders of the Chief Caretaker are never to be questioned.'

The argument was a powerful one and the Deputy had a lifetime of obedience behind him but he also knew that he had to break his habits if he was to survive. The strangeness of the Chief's appearance and the even greater strangeness of his remarks sent alarm bells ringing even in the Deputy's obtuse brain. He found himself edging past the Chief and towards the door talking frantically the while.

'Well, Chief,' he burbled, 'I think you may recall that there are certain cases specified in the rule book when Rule One, Paragraph One, Section One, can be over-ridden. And one of those occasions I think I'm right in saying is set out in Appendix K, Subsection 5X. And that's when the Chief Caretaker –'

'Yes?' The Deputy was at the door now but the Chief's question held him there suspended for a moment before he could break the spell.

Finally he blurted out the ruling: 'When the Chief Caretaker just isn't the Chief Caretaker . . .'

The Deputy turned and ran for his life through the open door out of the Headquarters. It would have been easy enough for the Cleaners to destroy him before he had got even an inch beyond the door but Kroagnon prevented them.

What was the point? What was the hurry? They would clean him up when they cleaned up all the others.

Mel and the Doctor sat on loungers beside the pool talking openly and honestly about their adventures as old friends can whenever they meet up. Nearby the Kangs, Blue and Red, now assembled up at the pool in the sky in full force, rested and gathered their strength for the final conflict. And some way off, Pex sat alone and unhappy, all too aware of the half-amused, half-contemptuous looks the Kangs occasionally gave him.

Mel had quickly alerted the Doctor and the Kangs to the dangers of the pool. Now she stared into it moodily.

'I'm sorry that you didn't really enjoy your swim, Mel,' the Doctor joked to cheer her up.

'Oh, it's all right,' Mel answered. 'I – we – finally shot whatever it was and the pool's been quiet since. But imagine building this beautiful pool and then filling it with mechanical killers.'

The Doctor sighed. 'The rest of the Towers would have been like this pool if the Great Architect had had his way. A killer in every corner.'

'And you're sure Kroagnon's been let loose again?' Mel enquired. They had been through the story already but Mel knew that they needed to keep going through it until the Doctor could see his way to some solution.

'Oh very much so.' The Doctor stroked his chin ruefully. 'But we know so little about his plans. That's what's so worrying. He's had years to brood over what he wants to do. We've no time at all to come up with the counterplan.'

His eyes wandered over to where Pex sat. Some of the Kangs had come up to him now and their mockery was more blatant.

'How's scaredy cat, Pex, then?' Bin Liner smirked.

Pex turned away in the vain hope that he might be left alone but Drinking Fountain cut in now. 'Did Mel make the creature unalive for you?' she jeered.

'And stop you being taken to the Cleaners?' put in Fire Escape.

Pex reluctantly admitted that this was the case. 'Then Mel *is* a Kang after all,' Fire Escape exclaimed thoughtfully. The other Kangs nodded. Pex was once again isolated, the only one who had not shown his bravery. And he resorted as usual to bluster.

'I'll show you all yet,' he proclaimed. 'I *will* put the world of Paradise Towers to rights.'

'Oh yes?' Bin Liner came closer and stared into Pex's face.

'Yes.' But Pex's bravado crumbled and he had to turn away.

'You're a cowardly cutlet,' Fire Escape announced triumphantly. 'When the in-betweens went to fight, you hid. You'll always hide. Always.'

And the three Kangs started a chant: 'He's a cowardly cutlet, he's a cowardly cutlet . . .'

Mel watched from afar in some distress. 'They shouldn't treat him like that.'

The Doctor patted her shoulder. 'What good will it do if you try to stop them?' But he too was depressed by what was happening. 'It's the problem of Paradise Towers in a nutshell,' he sighed. 'The Red Kangs didn't trust the Blue Kangs. None of them trust the Caretakers. The Rezzies, from your account, prey on whoever they can and trust no-one either. And all of them despise poor old Pex.' If Mel didn't know that the Doctor never despaired, she might have thought he was near despairing now. It all looked so bleak. 'The Great Architect must be delighted,' he added bitterly. 'How ever are we going to unite the people of Paradise Towers to defeat him?'

'He's a cowardly cutlet! He's a cowardly cutlet!'

The rest of the Kangs had joined in now and their mocking chant echoed round the swimming pool. Pex could bear it no longer. He got to his feet and started to walk away from his tormentors towards the main door of the pool.

Mel got to her feet and ran to him. 'Pex,' she called, 'don't go. Pex –'

But Pex had suddenly stopped half way to the exit. He stared ahead of him disbelievingly. Everyone else stared too, following his gaze. None of them could quite believe their eyes.

Maddy, the Rezzie, was standing at the entrance to the pool, her plump face anxious and her manner distinctively self-conscious as she felt the eyes of all the Kangs staring at her. Behind her stood a few other Residents, older and less vocal, sharing her embarrassment.

It took her a moment to find her voice.

'I – that is we, the Rezzies,' she began, nervously clearing her throat, 'the remaining Rezzies that is – wanted to talk to you.' She put out an appealing hand to her silent audience. 'I think – I think we may need your help.'

It was the Doctor who responded first. He had been close to despair and this was the first sign that there might be hope for the divided people of Paradise Towers. He came up to Maddy and raised his hat politely. Maddy responded with a grateful curtsey.

Then he led her into the pool area and helped her to a seat even though he was conscious all the time of the hostile scowls of the Kangs trained upon her. The other Rezzies trooped in obediently behind her, and, much to Mel's relief, Pex too decided to come back to hear what the Residents had to say.

At first Maddy spoke only in a disconnected and rather distraught way. Her timid soul lacked the toughness of Tilda and Tabby and what had been happening was almost too much for her.

'The Cleaners must have reached about Floor 115 by now,' she reported. The news caused consternation since their progress through the building was even swifter than any one had imagined. 'All the Rezzies who can have moved up to higher floors,' Maddy continued. Her face fell. 'Unfortunately not everyone was quick enough.'

The Doctor was thoughtful. 'And you're sure that the person ordering the Cleaners to do this looks like the Chief Caretaker.?'

Maddy nodded. If there had been any doubt before there could be none now. The Chief Caretaker was unalive but the Great Architect had used corpoelectroscopy to take over his body. No doubt for the Doctor anyway. The Kangs were not so sure.

'Why should we believe her?' Fire Escape pointed angrily at Maddy. 'Rezzies are full of untruths – and Kangs.'

The other Kangs joined in. It was a sudden outpouring of long-held grudges against the Rezzies and in particular the evil ways of Tilda and Tabby, deceased. The angry babble grew in power until finally the Doctor managed to calm them down by insisting on the importance of finding out all they could about what was happening. When the Kang protest had subsided to a murmur, the Doctor turned to Maddy and beckoned her to carry on.

Maddy took her courage in her hands and started to speak again, her hands twisting nervously. 'Of course, I know that we Residents have not always been as neighbourly as we might have been.' She cleared her throat again. 'But some have been worse than others and the worst have gone. Down the waste disposal chute.'

She stretched out her hands pleadingly, involving the other Rezzies in her plea. 'Those of us who are left want to let bygones be bygones. We're all in danger now and, well, we're very sorry for what we did. And we won't do it again. If we all survive that is.' Her anxious hands stretched out timidly to include all her hearers. 'We need each other's help.'

It was as handsome an apology as could be expected and the Doctor turned questioningly to the listening girls. 'Well, you Kangs,' he demanded, 'what do you say to that?'

The Kangs, Red and Blue, exchanged glances and then got into a huddle to consider their reaction. Maddy and the other Rezzies waited nervously for the verdict. Fortunately they did not have to wait too long. The huddle broke up and Bin Liner, who had obviously been nominated as the spokeswoman, turned to the Doctor.

'I won't say Rezzies are icehot,' she announced, 'but, yes she's not telling untruths and yes, we'll help each other.'

'Is that agreed?' The Doctor looked to the other Kangs and they nodded consent. Maddy smiled with relief and Mel started to feel the glimmer of hope growing within her.

'How about you, Pex?'

The Doctor was determined to get the whole group working together. No-one was to be excluded. The Kangs called Pex a cowardly cutlet again but the Doctor quietened them down and asked Pex again for his consent to work with the Rezzies. Embarrassed and unconfident though he was, he gave it.

'All right,' Fire Escape broke in impetuously, 'we work with Pex, no to-do, we work with Rezzies no to-do, but the Caretakers –'

'Never ever!' the Kangs cried vehemently in unison.

A new arrival coughed nervously. The conversation ceased and the assembled company craned to see who the newcomer was.

It was the Deputy Chief, looking incongruous and ill-at-ease in these surroundings. He spoke tentatively at first, conscious that he would be neither welcome nor trusted. But his haggard face and haunted eyes showed that the pompous Deputy had undergone experiences that had changed his very being.

'Excuse me –' he began, 'I'm sorry to intrude like this but I wondered if I might have a word with you all?'

Mel's eyes met the Doctor's. Much was still to be done but they had pulled themselves back from despair. They might still be able to win.

11

Kroagnon

Kroagnon was enjoying his freedom. The torture of confinement when his ever-fertile brain could only plan but not achieve was over. There had been times when he had even wished he might be allowed to die instead of being preserved in inactive torment. Not now. His revenge was working exactly according to plan and soon Paradise Towers would be his again.

In front of him in the Chief's control room he had a map laid out that showed a cross-section of the Towers. Above, the screens kept him informed of how far his Cleaners had progressed in their destruction of the human creatures. And, as each floor was reclaimed for his purposes, he crossed it through on the map with a blood-red pencil. Even he was surprised by how quickly his opponents fell back before him.

He realised, of course, that all the messy creatures were moving up to the Swimming Pool Zone on Floor 304. But, luckily for him, he didn't have to worry too much. They wouldn't have time to make it too untidy before he destroyed them.

A strange, cruel smile crossed Kroagnon's pallid features. He had nothing to fear, after all, had he? Nobody could know Paradise Towers better than the Great Architect who built it.

The Chief studied the screens for a while. The Cleaners were visible on all of them spraying clouds of noxious smoke. Another floor had fallen. One hundred and sixty three.

The absence of response was actually beginning to trouble Kroagnon's devious brain. Surely there would be *some* opposition? He decided that it was time to take a look for himself at what the human garbage were up to in the Swimming Pool Zone.

He pressed the appropriate buttons on the control panel and sat back to watch. But nothing happened. The screens all went blank. He pressed again. Still nothing happened.

And then a recorded voice spoke. And it gave Kroagnon no satisfaction to recognise it as his own, recorded just before the completion of the Towers: 'By express order of the Great Architect, Surveillance of the Swimming Pool is not allowed. Repeat. Not allowed.'

The Great Architect gave a hiss of disappointment. He remembered now that he had wanted to ensure that the crowning joy of his creation, the pool, would never be overlooked by prying human flesh. How could he have known that he himself would have need of an over-view of what was happening there one day?

It was annoying but not too serious a blow. It was simply curiosity that made him want to see what his enemies were up to. Not a very exalted emotion for such a brilliant brain. It was not as if their puny intellects could possibly come up with any way of stopping him.

'We don't have much time and we must think clearly. Kroagnon, as we must now call him, is firmly installed in your Headquarters.' The Doctor turned to the Deputy Chief for confirmation. 'Am I right?'

'Yes, Doctor.'

The Doctor sighed and scratched his brow. 'So we must find a way of getting him out again.'

'Set a trap for him,' Drinking Fountain put in.

'Precisely.' The Doctor looked round the assembled company. The poolside seating was occupied now by a motley collection of Kangs, Rezzies and Caretakers, all intent on finding a means of survival.

'We used to set traps for the rats,' Maddy began brightly but then, remembering Tilda and Tabby, she decided it wasn't a very tactful area to discuss and retreated, blushing, into silence.

'But what about the Cleaners?' Mel put in. Nobody had yet come up with any plan for dealing with them although everyone agreed that they had to be stopped. Indeed the Doctor had already said on several occasions during the discussion that as many of them as possible had to be immobilised. If the Cleaners could not be put out of action then what hope was there for defeating their master?

'Doctor –' the Deputy Chief spoke in the subdued silence that followed Mel's question, an idea apparently forming slowly in his brain.

'Yes, Deputy Chief?'

'Well, I know it goes against the rule book to say this but I suppose these are exceptional circumstances.'

'They might be described in that way, yes,' the Doctor agreed drily. The habits of a lifetime still pursued the Deputy, he noted, even when disaster stared him in the face.

The Deputy was now the centre of all attention and he knew it. 'Well,' he began nervously, 'on the 245th Floor Sodium Street Corridor 75, there is a Secret Emergency Supply kept in case of pests getting out of control –'

'An Emergency Supply of what?' Mel asked, expressing the puzzlement many felt.

'Explosive.'

'Icehot!' The Deputy's news brought an immediate enthusiastic response from Fire Escape and the Kangs.

'With explosives on our arrowguns, we could blow up the Cleaners no problem,' Bin Liner proclaimed cheerfully, waving her crossbow in the air.

'Send the Cleaners to the Cleaners!' Drinking Fountain added, sending all the Kangs into fits of glee. The Deputy smiled primly. He had never experienced popularity like this before. He knew he liked being liked but didn't yet know how to respond.

But now Maddy and the Rezzies were getting excited too. 'Most of the Rezzies make tablecloths,' Maddy said brightly to the Kang Leaders. 'We could throw them over the Cleaners to slow them down for you to shoot.'

'Icehot, Maddy!' The Kangs responded enthusiastically to this suggestion as well. Now there was a possibility of action, their high spirits were returning. Mel noticed sadly that only Pex was still not involved in the bustling, chatting, laughing group of people that now sat by the poolside.

The Doctor was pleased by this turn of events. The plan to get rid of the Cleaners showed they were getting somewhere at last. But his lightning-quick brain had already moved on to the next problem. It took him a while to calm the bubbling throng down but he eventually succeeded in getting their full attention.

'We ought to move on to the main problem,' he announced. 'How to persuade Kroagnon to leave his safety in the Caretakers' headquarters and come to a place of our choosing where we can trap and defeat him.'

His words acted like a bucket of cold water on the excitement. 'He'll never leave there until we are all wiped out,' the Deputy Chief returned gloomily. 'And we'll never manage to break in.' He sighed. 'I should know after all.'

No one spoke. No one made any suggestions. Just now the secondary problem had seemed soluble and people had quickly forgotten that as yet they had no way of destroying the primary one.

The Doctor, however, had not raised the problem to depress people. He did have an idea forming in his mind although he knew it was not foolproof. 'There is one way that might just work,' he told the group, sure now of their full concentration.

'What's that, Doctor?'

'Well,' the Doctor commenced, choosing his words very carefully, 'Kroagnon is undoubtedly a very clever and very proud being. And, like many clever and proud beings, he probably likes to be appreciated by his intellectual equals. Even better if once they have appreciated his cleverness, they can be outwitted and destroyed.' He paused to give his final words full force. 'I think if he had the chance of meeting such a person, he'd leave his lair to do so.'

Not surprisingly it was Mel, who knew the Doctor best, who

understood first. 'Doctor,' she protested, 'you're not going to–'

The Doctor held up a restraining hand to stop her. 'I've no choice, Mel. I mean, in all honesty, I think I am the only obvious candidate.'

'You'll go out there and show yourself and be killed?' she demanded.

'Oh no, no,' the Doctor answered swiftly. 'That would be extremely futile. I will allow myself to be seen. And then somebody else will go to Kroagnon and offer to lead him to me. Straight into our little trap. Now that person has a far more difficult and dangerous mission than I do.'

Everyone took in the Doctor's words and pondered his plan. For all its dangers, there was no doubt it was the best they had. It was Pex who ended the silence by coming forward.

'I will go to Kroagnon,' he proclaimed proudly. 'I am Pex and I am–'

'A cowardly cutlet,' put in Fire Escape cheekily. And all the Kangs laughed.

Pex turned on them angrily. 'You all have tasks to do. Caretakers, Rezzies, Kangs. Why should only Pex be left out?' He drew himself up proudly. 'Pex, the trained fighting machine, Pex the–'

'The scaredy cat.' It was Bin Liner who interrupted this time and now everyone was laughing at Pex's discomfiture. Apart, that is, from the Doctor and Mel. When they realised this, the others fell silent.

Mel looked Pex squarely in the face. She had seen his courage fail so many times that she could not be sure he was serious this time. And much was at stake. 'Pex,' she demanded sternly, 'are you sure you want to do this?'

But Pex's gaze did not flinch this time. His sincerity could not be doubted by anyone when he nodded his head to show his willingness to go.

'So be it then,' the Docor said quietly. The die was cast and there could be no going back.

The screens showed the Cleaners steadily continuing their

deadly work. Kroagnon crossed off another floor methodically on his plan of the Towers. Two hundred and thirteen floors all free of living flesh. He was already planning in his mind the magnificent redecoration he would initiate through the Cleaners once he had the building entirely to himself again. How much higher his imagination could soar when he no longer had the constraints of providing for dirty, noisy people to live and work in his masterpiece. Miracle City would be a plaything, a mere toy, compared with what he would achieve in Paradise Towers.

And then suddenly the reception faded on his central screen. And a strange face appeared. An intelligent face, it was true, but impish and insolent too with a batttered straw hat perched on its top. He stared at this visage on the screen, trying to place it. It was vaguely familiar but it was not someone with whom he had ever had dealings. Finally a hand came into view and raised the intruder's straw hat politely and then the face began to speak.

'Hello there, Kroagnon,' it began without any proper deference. 'This is the Doctor speaking. I don't believe we've met though no doubt you'll have heard of me.'

The Great Architect grunted savagely. The nerve of it! He may have heard of this Doctor, he may have not but that was hardly the point. The important thing surely was that the Doctor had heard of *him*.

'I thought you had,' the Doctor acknowledged cheerfully, guessing at the angry reaction at the other end. Despite not being able to see his auditor, he was beginning to enjoy his provoking role.

'Anyway,' he continued, 'I'd heard so much about Paradise Towers that I thought I'd come and take a look. And I have to say, I'm very disappointed. It displays exactly what everybody says is your usual failure as an architect. You don't make any allowances for people having to live in these places.' He smiled winningly in a way he hoped would have the Great Architect grinding his teeth in rage. 'Still, I'm sure if we manage to work together, you and I, we might just about manage to make this

132

place habitable.' The Doctor's face moved closer to the screen to whisper confidentially, 'I've one or two ideas I might give you if you could be bothered to listen. Bye for now.'

And, with another raising of his hat, the Doctor was gone. The screen went empty and a few seconds later the familiar images of the Cleaners at work returned. But Kroagnon no longer took them in.

The Great Architect sat there in a state of total fury. He had been so outraged by this upstart's impertinent remarks that he had even neglected to trace where the intruder had been located in the Towers while making his broadcast. But there would be time for revenge. Plenty of time. A few ideas to make things better! No allowances for people! Nobody ever criticised the Great Architect like that and lived to tell the tale.

One beneficial offshoot of the Doctor's perilous mission was that Kroagnon was too distracted with rage to monitor closely what was happening in the streets of the Towers. If he had, he would have had some nasty surprises. In Fountain of Happiness Square, for example, he would have seen a group of Red Kangs emerge from hiding to fire arrowgun shots loaded with explosives at passing Cleaners. And he would have seen them cheer as Cleaner after Cleaner was hit and then exploded.

He would have also seen scenes on the 209th floor which might have made him think that he had underestimated the elderly Rezzies. Maddy stood at one of the crossroads in wait for the Self-Activating Robots and when they came up she would step out and stop them.

'Excuse me,' she would say. 'I hope you don't mind my mentioning it but I think you've missed some rubbish in the street back there.' And she would point back the way the Cleaner had come. Thoroughly confused by the contradictory instructions, the Cleaner would turn slowly. And, as it did so, two other Rezzies would emerge from hiding and the Cleaner would be enveloped in a large knitted tablecloth unable to move or unleash its armoury of devices.

And then Drinking Fountain or one of the other Blues would appear and fire at the immobilised Cleaner. The loaded arrow would stick in its metal body. And then, when Rezzies and Kangs were safely out of range, the shot would explode and the Cleaner would be blown to pieces. Way past the point of repair even if anyone had wanted to repair it.

A great number of Cleaners were disposed of in scenes like this. But there was even more frantic activity back at the Red Kang Brainquarters. This had been selected as the centre of the trap that was to be baited for the Great Architect. Inside, Kangs and Caretakers scurried around like ants stacking into every available nook and cranny in the room the rest of the explosive from the store on the 245th Floor. Soon it would be like a huge bomb needing only the right detonator to explode. And up the steps on ground level the Deputy Chief and Fire Escape were at work on that detonator – a complex mechanism that had to be built into the structure of the replacement entry door.

In the midst of all this, Pex, pale but collected, was receiving his final briefing from the Doctor and Mel.

'You're clear now what you have to do, Pex?' the Doctor enquired.

'And you're sure you want to go through with it?' Mel added, earnestly.

Pex nodded, his square jaw set. 'I won't be unbrave again,' he reassured them.

'The main thing to remember,' the Doctor advised, 'is to get him out of the Caretakers' Headquarters as soon as possible so he doesn't see what is happening to the Cleaners. We've been lucky on that so far but our luck won't last for ever.' Then the Doctor repeated once more the crucial part of the plan. 'Remember, though, once he's out, take as long as you can to get him here. Preparing all this is difficult and dangerous work and we need as much time as you can gain us.' He put his hand on Pex's shoulder to re-enforce the point. 'No heroics, Pex. Just a cool, clear head.'

'I can manage.' Pex was very different now his mind was

made up. He talked less and listened more. Impressed, the Doctor shook his hand and wished him well.

And then it was Mel's turn. She had grown very fond of Pex for all his idiocies and she hated to think this might be their last conversation. She tried not to think of that, though, and luckily for her, she had something to give him that took her mind off the danger. It was a Kang bracelet.

'They wanted to give it to you, Pex.' Mel explained as she fastened it round his neck. 'They think you're not a scaredy cat any longer but a real Kang.' And she kissed the blushing Pex gently on the cheek. 'Good luck, Pex.'

He stood awkwardly for a moment and then reached into his belt. He pulled out his gun and handed it to Mel. 'You take this, Mel,' he mumbled. 'I can't use it this time.'

It was all Pex had to give and Mel was touched. Soon he was gone and she was left to think over what would happen to him. He was right, of course. His gun would be worse than useless in the encounter Pex had ahead of him. He would need clear-headedness and courage far more. She could only hope that Pex had really discovered those qualities in himself. If he hadn't then it boded ill for their whole undertaking.

With a sigh, Mel went to help the others with preparation of the door. The Doctor had not exaggerated. They would need every second Pex could buy them.

The Great Architect had spent precious time trying to trace the impertinent Doctor but without success. He should not have allowed himself to become so angered. It was not fitting for an intellect of his capacity. But if there was one thing he could not endure, it was any suggestion that his architectural design was less than perfect. He began making plans for a particularly nasty contraption in which the Doctor would be incarcerated and slowly crushed.

Still, he should make sure how his Cleaners were getting on first. They should at least be up to the 260th floor by now. He pressed the control buttons to take a look. And to his surprise a face appeared again on the central screen. A different face

135

though. A young warrior by the look of him, strong-jawed and powerful, but with absolutely no intellectual capacity whatsoever. Still, it could do no harm to listen to what he had to say.

Pex was sweating. He could not help it. But still he managed to hold his ground and get his story out. He was a disillusioned rebel against Kroagnon. He had been treated badly by the arrogant Doctor and wanted revenge.

'So you could lead me to this Doctor, could you?' asked the sinister metallic voice softly, terrifying Pex to the marrow.

'Yes,' he answered as firmly as he could. 'He and the other remaining – er – mobile rubbish have found a place to hide which they think you don't know about. And they're planning ways of resistance.'

The Great Architect smiled secretly. Taking these meddlers by surprise like rats in a trap appealed to his sense of humour. It was so much more amusing than sitting around here in the Caretakers' Headquarters while the Cleaners had all the fun.

One doubt remained. 'Why should you help Kroagnon?' he asked the warrior.

But Pex had been prepared to answer this question. 'Because I don't belong with the others here,' he explained. 'I know you're going to win. All I ask is that you promise me a safe way out of the Towers when the others are destroyed.'

'Of course,' Kroagnon returned smoothly. 'If you deliver me the Doctor, I'll give you a safe way out.' He smiled again. It was so easy to make promises when you had no intention of keeping them.

'Doctor!' Mel ran down the steep steps of the Brainquarters. She found him checking out the layout of the explosive. 'Doctor,' she gasped breathlessly, 'the door's nearly in place. But they're having a problem with the fortimoloscope opening device.'

The Doctor looked grave. This device was the key to the whole ambush. Triggered by the slightest touch it would make the door spring open and catapult the intended victim into the

136

explosive below. Half a minute later it would also trigger the explosive itself. If it did not work, the plan was sunk. 'I'd better give them a hand,' the Doctor decided. 'See what you can do to help the Kangs down here, Mel,' he added. 'And don't forget to leave the secret escape hatch uncovered so that I can make my exit.'

Everything depended on split-second timing. The door was to spring open. The Great Architect was to see the Doctor below. He would lean down to see him. Pex would push him from behind. And the Great Architect would topple to his death a split-second after the Doctor had sneaked to safety from the exploding Brainquarters.

'I just hope Pex doesn't lose his nerve and hurry,' the Doctor muttered to himself as he rushed up the steps. 'Otherwise it won't be Kroagnon who's caught in a booby trap. It'll be us.'

They had been the most terrifying minutes of Pex's life. First the talk with Kroagnon. Then the wait for him to emerge from the Headquarters to join Pex at the appointed place with a flotilla of Cleaners in tow. And now, worst of all, the slow progress along the familiar streets and squares of the Towers with the Great Architect by his side, his fearsome red eyes darting this way and that, his measured robotic tread telling of ferocious power and determination.

Pex knew that concealed along the way were Kangs with crossbows. But he also knew that they could only observe what was happening not intervene. If they were lucky, they might be able to pick off a few of the Cleaners with their explosive during the final moments. But Kroagnon was far too wily to put himself in any position where he might be exposed to danger from hidden enemies.

'This is not some trick, is it?' the Great Architect demanded as they walked side by side. His wolfish grin made Pex's blood run cold.

'No, no,' Pex answered, feeling his heart pounding faster and faster.

'That's just as well,' leered Kroagnon. 'I've only just begun to enjoy walking round my marvellous Towers again in this body. And I wouldn't deal kindly with anyone who was stupid enough to try and lay a trap for me.'

He stopped suddenly and his eyes pierced into Pex's. Their brilliance and cruelty were quite breath-taking. Pex felt he could hide nothing from such a being. Kroagnon edged closer. 'Not frightened, are you?' he hissed.

It was too much. Pex knew his nerves would not hold. This awful ordeal had to end as soon as possible. 'I think . . . I think we ought to hurry, Great Architect,' Pex begged. 'Please – let's hurry.' He hated himself for saying it but he was convinced he would blurt out everything if he had to stare into those deep eyes one second longer.

'As you wish,' the Great Architect replied, a trace of cruel amusement entering his face at Pex's terror. And he quickened his pace to match Pex's.

Drinking Fountain, hidden nearby, watched this development with dismay. If they kept up this pace they would be there far, far too soon. She hurried to the nearest talkiphone to report.

It was Bin Liner who took the call in the Brainquarters. Most of the Kangs had already left the explosive-lined room but she and Mel were still there to await the notification of Kroagnon's arrival.

'What's happened?' Mel asked anxiously as she saw Bin Liner's face cloud over with dismay.

'They're making all speed here,' Bin Liner replied.

'What?' Mel could not believe the awfulness of the news.

'Pex has been a scaredy cat,' Bin Liner continued bitterly replacing the talkiphone receiver. 'They'll be here in no time.

'I must warn the Doctor.' Mel started to run up the stairs to where he was working. But Bin Liner stopped her just in time. As an added precaution, trip wires had been laid. One step up the stairs and Mel would have gone up in smoke. And the plan with her. She had no choice but to follow Bin Liner through the secret escape hatch. In her agony, she realised there was nothing else she could do to help the Doctor.

The fortimoloscope opening device had proved tricky even for the Doctor and valuable minutes had ticked away while he had been working on it. But now he finally thought he had got it working.

'Doctor –' The Deputy Chief's voice was suddenly stiff with fear. They looked up the street and what they saw was the last thing they wanted to see. The Great Architect had turned the corner and was coming towards them with Pex at his side.

'And we're not ready for them.' In those few simple words the Deputy had expressed it all. Pex had failed them when the Doctor had trusted him. The plan was ruined and the Doctor would have to make do as best he could.

The first thing he did was to persuade the Deputy and Fire Escape to move back away from the door. They were reluctant to do so, particularly the Red Kang leader who did not want to abandon her teacher to certain death. 'But you must go,' the Doctor insisted urgently. 'There's only one way this might work. And for that I need to be on my own.'

Finally they withdrew. And the Doctor, totally alone by the door, turned to face his approaching enemy. Seeing the Doctor was alone, Kroagnon gestured to his cohorts of Cleaners to wait at the end of the street. He advanced himself, however, a triumphant smile on his lips and a quivering Pex by his side.

They came nearer and nearer but the Doctor held his ground. And Mel and Bin Liner emerged into the street from the secret escape route to join the small frightened group that clustered at the corner of the street some way behind the Doctor's back. Mel had imagined the Great Architect would be alarming. But she had never imagined anyone as terrifying as this grisly corpse-like creature who towered over her Doctor.

'Well?'

The Doctor's careful plans were in ruins. All he could do was improvise in the faint hope that an opportunity might occur for him to push Kroagnon single-handed through the barely completed door into the blackness below. The Doctor, however, was a creature of enormous determination and resource. He assumed a cheerful expression and started to chatter away as if nothing untoward had happened.

'Well, well, Kroagnon,' he started as the Great Architect approached, 'how nice of you to drop in. I'm so glad. I wanted to have a few words with you about the shoddy design of this building.' He gestured towards the door, hoping desperately his foe would not notice its newness. 'I mean, take a look at this for instance.'

Kroagnon glowered. 'There was nothing wrong with it when I built it,' he roared. 'Unless humanoid creatures have damaged it.'

'Well, speaking as an expert,' the Doctor proclaimed, trying to draw the Great Architect nearer to the object under discussion, 'I'm prepared to tell the Universe you couldn't design a simple door knob. Look at it.'

Curiosity and vanity got the better of Kroagnon and he moved towards the door to examine it more closely and defend his workmanship. It was the Doctor's chance. Swiftly he operated the fortimoloscope device, the door flew open and he tried to push the Great Architect down.

Kroagnon nearly fell but at the last minute he managed to stop himself. And then he grabbed at the Doctor and held him tight. A terrific fight took place upon the edge of an opening that lead to a ferocious booby trap. And though the Doctor struggled gallantly, there was no doubt that the other was the stronger and would in time prevail.

Pex, the only person near at hand, watched, horrified. The Doctor called for him to help but it was hopeless. He could no more take action than he could by the side of the great Pool in the Sky. Whatever courage he had managed to acquire had vanished quite away. In fact, it was worse than before. For now Pex started to run from the desperate struggle as fast as he could, abandoning the Doctor to be bruised and buffeted before being thrown to his death.

He ran first towards the Cleaners but realised quickly there could be no escape that way. So he ran the other way towards where the tight little group of Mel, the Deputy and the Kangs watched helplessly.

And then Pex's eyes met those of Mel. And there was such reproach in her eyes for betraying her Doctor that he could not stand it. Pex fingered the bracelet the Kangs had given him. The sign that he was indeed part of Paradise Towers not an outcast and a laughing stock. Mel was still staring at him with a beseeching look in her eye and in a moment all the memories of their adventures together flooded back into his agitated brain.

To Pex the debate in his brain took an age to resolve itself. To the watchers it was all a matter of seconds. He stood there irresolute for a moment, fingered his bracelet, exchanged a final glance of understanding with Mel and rushed back to the fight.

The Doctor was at his last gasp, barely aware of what was happening, when Pex pushed him aside. Dimly he became aware that Pex was grappling with Kroagnon in a fierce and deadly struggle and that he could now step back for a moment to draw breath.

He collapsed with a gasp on the floor nearby. And, as he did so, Pex gave a final triumphant cry and jumped back into the darkness dragging the struggling Kroagnon with him.

A few seconds later there was a huge explosion. The trap had achieved its purpose. But at a cost.

12

Farewells

The shrine the Kangs built was a simple one. Improvised from the rubbish of Paradise Towers as the shrines of unalive Kangs had been in the past. But on the top of it they placed Pex's gun, a last reminder of the saviour of the Towers.

Bin Liner led the ceremony in a quiet and dignified way. The words Mel had heard once for the last of the Yellow Kangs echoed in her brain now. But this time a Kang leader was standing in Fountain of Happiness Square before a solemn assembly of all the residents of Paradise Towers. Not just the Red Kangs and the Blue Kangs. But Maddy and the Rezzies. And the Deputy Chief Caretaker with all the remaining Caretakers.

'Hail Pex.' Bin Liner's young voice echoed eloquently round the Square. 'Hail the unalive who gave his life for the Towers. In life he was not a Kang but in death he was brave and bold as a Kang should be.'

'Hail Pex. Hail the unalive . . . '

Other voices took up the chant now, circling reverently round the shrine as they did so. Mel and the Doctor watched slightly apart from the others. Though as moved as the celebrants, they somehow felt themselves not part of what was going on. After all, they did not belong to Paradise Towers.

'Poor Pex,' Mel sighed sadly.

'Indeed, poor Pex,' agreed the Doctor comfortingly. 'But look, Mel, they are all here. Caretakers. Rezzies. Kangs. That would never have happened before. Perhaps now they will all start working together.'

' . . . in death he was brave and bold as a Kang should be. Hail Pex . . . '

Fire Escape and Drinking Fountain came up to the Doctor and Mel. They were not yet part of the ceremony because they had had a more pressing task. Removing the Kang wallscrawl from the TARDIS. They reported that the job was now done. The Doctor and Mel could finally depart.

'Build High for Happiness, Doctor.' Fire Escape gave the Kang salute and then handed the Doctor a timely farewell present. His much battered brolly which had been found when Kangs and Caretakers had been cleaning out the Basement.

'We are sorry you must go, Doctor – and Mel,' Drinking Fountain blurted out, still awkward at admitting the affection she felt for them. She held up a blue sash. 'We have made you an Honorary Kang, Doctor.'

The Doctor smiled and regarded the sash. 'A Blue Kang or a Red Kang?'

'Both.' Grinning, Fire Escape took the sash from Drinking Fountain and showed that its reverse was coloured red.

'In that case,' the Doctor replied, placing the sash around his neck, 'I will be honoured to wear it.'

In the background the chanting continued. Soon Fire Escape and Drinking Fountain would join the others. The Doctor and Mel took one last look round Fountain of Happiness Square and then they knew it was time to go.

'All my best wishes for the future of Paradise Towers!' the Doctor called as he and Mel entered the TARDIS. The two Kangs waved farewell and then melted into the disparate group still celebrating their first communal act.

A second later the TARDIS had dematerialised – revealing on the wall behind where it had stood a brand-new Kang wallscrawl. There had been more elaborate wallscrawls before but few as heartfelt. It showed a picture of Pex's weapon over a Red Kang sash and a Blue Kang sash interlinked. And underneath the two words:

PEX LIVES.

THIS OFFER EXCLUSIVE TO

READERS

**Pin up magnificent full colour posters of
DOCTOR WHO**

**Just send £2.50 for the first poster and £1.25
for each additional poster**

TO: PUBLICITY DEPARTMENT *
   W. H. ALLEN & CO PLC
   44 HILL STREET
   LONDON W1X 8LB

Cheques, Postal Orders made payable to WH Allen PLC

POSTER 1 ☐   POSTER 2 ☐   POSTER 3 ☐
POSTER 4 ☐   POSTER 5 ☐

Please allow 28 DAYS for delivery.

I enclose £ _____

CHEQUE NO. _____

ACCESS, VISA CARD NO. _____

Name _____

Address _____

_____

_____